go for
-it!

AIR LINE TICKET

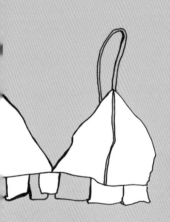

THE
NEW
GIRL
CODE

Niki Smit

THE NEW GIRL CODE

the launch of a fashion app

GIRL

CODE

Edited by Andrea Stanley

The New Girl Code is also available in South Africa. In the Netherlands, Sweden, and the United Kingdom the book is available as Project Prep.

Profit from this book supports Inspiring Fifty, an initiative increasing diversity in tech by making female role models in tech more visible.

First Edition, 2018.
ISBN 978-90-829271-0-8

hello@thenewgirlcode.com

#SocialMedia

www.thenewgirlcode.com

@thenewgirlcode   @thenewgirlcode

#thenewgirlcode

follow for inspiration, coding, fashion, and so much more

The New Girl Code is an initiative of

Inspiring Fifty

#Thenewgirlcode

Did you love reading *The New Girl Code?* Please share it with a friend.
Write them an inspiring message and pass it on!

if somebody judges me, then they're not my people, and that's all right

Constance Wu

#Basic

Friday, August 25

3:02 p.m.

20 Facts About Me:

1. I'm 15.
2. My name is Charlie.
3. Nine out of 10 times people think Charlie is a boy.
4. I live in Brooklyn but not the cool part.
5. I have a mom, dad, and an older brother named Finn.
6. I live in all-white Converse.
7. I like things that are different from a typical high school girl.
8. I think coding is cool.
9. I taught myself a few basics on how to code.
10. I am thinking about joining the coding club.
11. I am not great at taking selfies.
12. I am starting my sophomore year of high school in 3 days!
13. So far, high school has been take it or leave it, nothing horrible but nothing special.
14. Out of all my classes I thrive in math the most.
15. I think my dream job is something in technology.
16. But I tell everyone I haven't figured out what I want to do yet. And I guess that's kind of true.
17. Michelle Obama is my feminist hero.
18. Emma is my best friend and my fashion style icon.
19. I obsess over my insecurities.
20. I wish I were Emma.

Emma is my best friend. She's also annoyingly perfect. She has long reddish hair that never looks frizzy—even after getting sweaty in gym class. She's probably the future prom queen—actually, probably the future freaking president of the United States. I only say she's annoyingly perfect because next to her I always feel invisible. We can both wear the same sneakers, white tee, and messy topknot, and somehow I look like I just rolled out of bed and she looks flawless.

Sometimes I wonder if I met Emma when we were in high school if we would have become friends. I'm easy to miss, which in high school is both wonderfully beneficial and sadly soul-crushing at the same time. But I'll never know because we met in kindergarten—bonded over a shared love of animal crackers and Dr. Seuss books—and have been BFFs ever since.

Recently Emma posted a #TBT photo of us that shows what I mean. It was the summer after kindergarten on a family trip at the beach. She's wearing a striped one-piece bathing suit and standing next to a sandcastle just higher than her ankles. It's decorated with pink stones and starfish stencil imprints. I'm to the right in the frame, almost like a shadow in the picture—faded, yet there, but not in a significant way. I'm in a swimsuit that's ill-fitting, even for a five-year-old, and it looks like I spilled an electric-red drink down the front of it. My sandcastle has been partly washed away by the foamy water, and what remains of it is less castle and more clump. I have a giant smile on my face. I'm guessing it's because I didn't know then what perfect looked like. In that moment, I probably believed it was me. But I know now—and it's not.

It's Emma.

7:43 p.m.

I'm on the C train on my way back to Brooklyn after shopping with Emma that didn't go so well. I have that feeling when everyone around me looks so happy that I just want to scream.

I had hoped that somehow the shopping trip would kick off a metamorphosis, that I would magically become better and prettier than I was in the last school year. Apparently that happens for some girls—all it takes is a 90-day summer break, a different haircut, and a new outfit to become someone entirely new and worthy of being popular.

So when Emma invited me to go and pick out new outfits, I had hoped that somehow *that* would be the thing that sparked my transformation, my metamorphosis. That maybe if I just changed my outfit to a pair of millennial pink or Gen Z yellow overalls it would change me on a deeper level, too. I guess

I always knew that wouldn't be true, but that didn't stop me from secretly hoping that it *could* be true.

Here's what actually happened: I took the C train to Soho. The plan was for me to meet Emma there because she was already in the city visiting her aunt. I love Soho. It has really cool graffiti and cobblestoned streets that make me feel like I'm in an episode of *Gossip Girl*. Emma loves it because of the amazing shopping.

When I met up with her, she explained that we were on a mission to find things that were "next-level," "fierce," and that would make it look like we had "cool-girl style." I wasn't really sure what that meant. But this was before the letdown of realizing that there would be no summer-break transformation— so I was still feeling excited. We stopped at Cha Cha Matcha and got iced green tea matchas, took selfies in front of a white wall painted with rainbow-colored hearts, and then hit up some stores.

We started at What Goes Around Comes Around, a thrift boutique that has the best old-school Levi jeans. The store smells like old photographs and I almost felt like I was digging through my grandmother's closet, except for the fact that the girl who worked there was the kind of cool that made me feel awkward to be around. In other words, the high school metamorphosis for her was real. I compare every inch of myself to her. I try not to stare—but totally stare—at her perfect eyeliner, tiny chain necklaces, and an off-the-shoulder crop top. As she folds shirts, I see that her navy blue nail polish has a slight chip—a flaw! But upon looking again, even that looks like an intentional part of her chill vibe. She's an in-the-flesh reminder of what pretty looks like.

Before I can dwell on it any longer, Emma is ready to go. We head to some of her other favorite places to find new trends, like Brandy Melville, Forever 21, and Urban Outfitters.

Emma crushed it. She got frayed denim, sweatshirts with oversized sleeves, velvet ankle booties, metallic skirts, and a leather backpack. I tried on the same stuff in the dressing room and as much as I tried to convince myself that I looked okay—maybe even good—I realized I just looked, well, ridiculous. In one of the stores, Emma convinced me to try on a cropped puffer jacket. Apparently that style is a thing—but it must not be my thing. I felt like I was squeezing into a coat from when I was in third grade.

When I hopped on the subway to head home, I was empty-handed and full of tears—the kind that sting if you try to keep them in your eyes and taste salty when you eventually blink and they fall to your lips. I was alone. Emma had gone to get her haircut, and even though she had invited me to go, my mom said there was no way she was going to spend $120 on what would "barely be a trim." Now I'm going to show up to school on the first day with split ends, which never even crossed my mind before, but now suddenly feels like the end of the world.

Whatever. Next to Emma, I'm basically invisible anyway.

What does it mean if you're always comparing yourself to your friend piece-by-piece, freckle-by-freckle, word-by-word?

8:08 p.m.

Okay, so the shopping trip is something I'd like to forget, but thankfully, I just remembered something important: I need to sign up for my school's coding club. I have been going back and forth about whether I should do it. There are cons: It's almost all boys plus all of my friends are signing up for soccer, which happens to be at the same time and we agreed to do it together. And did I mention it's all boys? And there's really only one pro: It makes me happy. That doesn't feel like enough.

But after thinking about it, I realize that I *can't* stop thinking about it, which seems like a sign that I need to do it. There is a risk that I'll end up being known as the nerd whose best friend is a computer, but that's no worse than being the girl who doesn't even know how to kick a soccer ball. And hello, changing in front of everyone in the locker room? Mortifying! Especially since my mom refuses to let me wear anything but a white training bra ("fancy undergarments are not for girls your age," she says). And honestly, the fact that it makes me happy *is* enough! So coding club it is.

I've never taken a *real* computer language course before, and I'm excited to up my skills. The idea gives me butterflies, the good kind. I've always been creative, but not in the art, singing, or writing kind of way. But at camp last summer there was a STEM session, and I loved how creative writing lines of code made me feel. I didn't know technology could do that—but it can. Since then, I've tried to teach myself more through online courses, but it's been a little slow.

I'm in the middle of trying to figure out the password to my school account when I see a message from Emma. Seeing her name reminds me that I have to explain to her why I'm not signing up for soccer now.

EMMA: U there?

ME: *Yeah.*

EMMA: My new haircut turned out sooooo good. But now I'm trying to decide how to wear it on the first day. Google fishtail braid. Do u like it?

ME: Wut?!?! Looks hard to do!

EMMA: I watched a YouTube video. It's easy.

This was Emma—plotting *her* first-day comeback. I feel panicked. Maybe I do need to figure out how to up my style game. I Google fishtail braid (it does look hard, by the way) and fall down the rabbit hole of some of my favorite fashion influencers. I go back to searching online and there it is: "How to Have Cool-Girl Style." I click on the article and quickly read the tips:

1. **Forget about being perfect.** An effortless street-style vibe is pulled off by looking chill. If you're wearing a button-down top, scrunch up the sleeves and tuck in only one side of the shirt or mix patterns that are unexpected.

2. **Have a signature item.** Go for a few dainty gold necklaces worn at different lengths, a classic watch that you wear face in, or a neutral-colored, cross-body bag. Whatever you do, don't wear them all at the same time—you'll look like a try-hard.

3. **Go low.** Looking overdone is not the goal. Throw on sneakers with a dressy top.

4. **Don't always follow the trends.** If you love this season's chunky sweaters with exaggerated sleeves, go for it! But don't load up your closet with too many of-the-moment pieces. Wear the classics, too.

5. **Own it. Clothes are all about attitude.** Do you, and everyone will take notice.

I guess moods are like the weather—always changing. Because it feels like I've got this. I just need to make a list of what I need. Here's what I've come up with:

- Tie-front top
- Something in velvet...
- ...And maybe something in plaid—but definitely something in velvet
- Cropped jeans
- A faux fur multicolored vest
- A plain white tee (to wear with the vest)
- A few long, gold layering necklaces
- Track pants (but only maybe)
- Bomber jacket (the kind that sits on your shoulders and somehow stays in place)
- Leather backpack
- Black ankle boots that are tight at the ankle

I have saved up almost three months of allowance from babysitting over the summer. That should be enough to get everything. Plan B: I'll wait on the track pants.

9:09 p.m.

My password! I remember now! I changed it at the end of freshman year to *beachbound2018* because Emma and I were going on a trip to Fire Island.

I type it in and finally get into the school portal, but somehow the coding club is completely full. I hit the enter button again hoping that somehow it was a technological glitch and that my computer got it all wrong. But no: *Club at capacity.* The sudden onset of weepy sadness just as quickly smeared into annoyed anger. Since when did technology become the hottest club at school?

9:35 p.m.

I'm second-guessing everything.

You know what's harder than figuring out what classes or extracurricular activities to take sophomore year? Trying to figure out what to do with your life. Emma has everything mapped out. She's going to become a fashion stylist. She wants to intern in either Milan or Paris, and then she's going to move back to New York and work for Alexander Wang. I can see exactly what her life will look like—foamy coffees, fancy lunches, an apartment with views of the Empire State Building, and airline tickets that list destinations almost too exotic to pronounce.

The symbolism in that #TBT picture Emma posted of us at the beach juts out at me (my English teacher would be so proud). Just like my sandcastle, our friendship feels as if it's built on an unsteady foundation, and that when the truth eventually shakes out—that I'm not good enough for Emma who only gets more popular—our friendship will crumble (my English teacher would be so, so proud). I'm just a filler (BFF = Best Filler Friend) until her forever comes. And now that we're almost sophomores, we're one year closer to forever—or at least real life after high school.

As for me and my future, I don't know if I'll live in New York or not—I definitely won't be living in a lame section of Brooklyn. The only thing I've ever felt drawn to is something with computers. I'd love to develop an app or possibly run my own tech company. But if I don't get involved in any STEM clubs or take some technology classes, how am I going to get into a good college for coding?

I'm bummed, because I realize it was never cool-girl style that was going to give me my metamorphosis (even if only for myself)—it was the coding club.

Club at capacity.

11:30 p.m.

I'm trying to fall asleep but everyone is rapidly trying to keep their Snapchat streaks going, so my phone is constantly buzzing. I open the screen and see that I have 13 new Snaps. Probably all selfies. I roll over, pull my light-purple blanket up to my nose and try to fall asleep. Eventually, I do. But first I think about: *Will the next social media app be developed by a girl? Am I ever going to be able to convince my mom to buy me that Longchamp bag? Is Emma going to be in at least half of my classes? Should I just sign up for the soccer team?*

Saturday, August 26

9:03 a.m.

I wake up to a text from Emma. It's a photo of her new jean jacket. She says it cost only $6 because she found it a local thrift store in Brooklyn. I watch her Snapchat story and see that she personalized it by adding a bunch of varsity patches to the denim. Amazing. I respond back that I love it and ask if she wants to go shopping again. I'm torn on why I'm even asking. I know an outfit isn't going to make me feel better, but going through the motions feels like a better move than hiding out in my room.

9:05 a.m.

Emma's out. She has to go her little sister's music recital later.

The worst news? Looks like I'm going to have to ask my mom if she'll take me. But the good news? Maybe she'll splurge on that bag.

11:00 a.m.

My mom is totally into the idea of a trip to downtown NYC so I can pick up some outfits for school, but she decides to invite the whole family to go. Now I'm stuck hanging with my mom *and* my dad, plus my older brother, Finn, all day.

Finn is two years older than I am. You'd think that having an older brother would have its advantages, like getting to hang out with his cool friends or going to parties with seniors. But, no. He hangs out alone in his room all day. I guess he's playing video games or texting with his friends. But I'm only guessing. The extent of most of our conversations is "pass the cereal" as we eat breakfast in the morning.

12:59 p.m.

We're walking down Prince Street when my dad announces that he and my brother are going to check out a massage chair store. "A free muscle relaxation session," he says. It's dorky and lame and makes me wish that Emma's sister didn't have a music recital.

With my dad and Finn gone, my mom and I wait at the crosswalk for the light to change. It smells like salty pretzels and charring meat from a nearby food vendor. The air is hot and sticky (a passing tourist declares it "swampy"). We turn onto West Broadway and head toward H&M.

1:36 p.m.

I have an armful of stuff and my mom sends me back to the fitting room. Nothing looks right.

I need Emma.

My mom comes back with a chunky sweater that looks sort of cropped in the front and longer in the back. I text Emma a pic.

"Perfectly slouchy," she responds.

Even my mom is better at this than I am.

I still spend ten minutes checking myself out in the mirror. My mom calls over the door that it's on fleek and that we need to get going to lunch—my dad and Finn are waiting for us. I hate when my mom tries to talk like she's my age.

I get the sweater.

And I actually feel better.

1:47 p.m.

I wanted to go to the coffee stand at Nickel and Diner—the monochromatic décor would look perfect on my feed. Plus it's not far from the Audrey Hepburn street mural I've been wanting to see. But my mom says it's too late for pastries and lattes and that we need "a real lunch." So we end up at The Dutch.

My mom can go overboard when it comes to family outings. She works at New York University researching the effects of pollution on our society. Her days are long during the week, which means she hogs our time a lot on the weekend and forces us all to hang out.

As my dad orders us some sort of cheese appetizer, I refresh my feed. Two girls I know from school are at Nickel and Diner.

6:59 p.m.

On the way home, we make a few more stops. I end up with a striped blazer, velvet flats, boyfriend jeans, a slouchy white tee, and some gold stackable rings from an adorable boutique we pass by in Brooklyn called Catbird.

Feeling even better.

10:56 a.m.

I'm bored. I've already read through the first chapter of my new math book. I watched 111 Snapchat Stories. I'm considering whether I should email the coding club teacher to see if there's some way I can still get in.

But then a text from Emma.

EMMA: Want to chill one more time before we have to go back to school?

ME: Sure. My place at 2?

EMMA: K. See you then.

7:13 p.m.

Maybe I'm being dramatic about the whole being a filler friend thing and comparing my friendship with Emma to a crumbling sandcastle.

When she shows up to my house, she's the one freaking out about how I was going to be the one who outgrows her. "We have a lot of different classes, so you could make an entirely new group of friends," she says.

"Never, Emma," I tell her. I'm trying to convince her—but really I'm trying to convince myself.

There are just a few hours of summer left. Maybe everything will change, maybe it won't. It's impossible to know. But for now, we watch *Mean Girls* and then Emma helps me put together my looks for the first few weeks of school. She creates 12 different combinations for me to wear.

BFF = Best Filler Friend.

BFF = Best Friend Forever.

7:01 a.m.

There's just over an hour until homeroom. I put on one of the outfits that Emma came up with for me. I wouldn't exactly call it a metamorphosis.

Actually, I feel a little off in my oversized

shirt. The sleeves balloon in ways that make me feel small and insignificant. Not exactly ideal first-day vibes. I debate changing, but Emma texts me that she's waiting outside to walk with me to school. So I grab my bag and dash out the door.

8:29 a.m.

The first thing Emma and I see when we get to school are a bunch of upperclassmen. As they look our way, I don't feel small and insignificant anymore in my shirt—I feel awkwardly big and like my sleeves are taking up too much space. I bump into a senior boy and blush. Emma and I have homeroom together, so that at least makes me feel better.

10:45 a.m.

It's third period and I'm still thinking about what happened in homeroom. Emma and I didn't get to sit next to each other. The teacher put names in a hat and made us sit with whosoever name was pulled out at the same time as ours.

Emma ended up sitting next to a girl named Aisha, and I was paired up with a girl named River. She was wearing boyfriend-style black pants, red track sneakers, and a cropped gray sweater.

I tried to make conversation with her but she just kind of nodded and sort of smiled but didn't say anything.

Emma spent the entire homeroom laughing with Aisha, who has beautiful curly hair and curves that make me feel like a little girl.

4:03 p.m.

I'm home from school and like I predicted, there was no metamorphosis. Even crappier news: Emma invited Aisha to sit with us during lunch. The truth is, I don't not like Aisha. If I'm being honest, she seems pretty cool. It's more that I'm worried she seems cooler than me and maybe Emma will start thinking that, too. Aisha spent most of the time telling us how she moved to Brooklyn three years ago from Miami after her parents divorced. Her dad is an international businessman and travels to Europe frequently. She loves the shows *Stranger Things* and *Riverdale*.

Emma invited her to join us the next day for soccer tryouts.

Suddenly I was in a 3FF situation (3FF = 3 Friends Forever).

I knew it was coming. But Emma making new friends right in front of me felt like watching your crush make out with someone else—a really twisted kind of heartbreak. Raw, vulnerable, and hurtful.

10:08 p.m.
I had three hours of stuff to do just on Day One.

I'm exhausted.

I see a text pop up on my phone that at first looks like it's Emma—but then I see Aisha is included, too. Now we're group texting?

I click off my phone.

Then I click it back on to search: "How to be the favorite friend?" The advice isn't great and is all about being yourself—but that's the problem.

Tuesday, August 29

7:02 a.m.
I'm up and dressed in under five minutes. I heart Emma for helping me get all of my looks together. I feel a little guilty for not responding to the group text last night. I pull up the thread with Emma and Aisha.

"Good morning," I type out. And follow up quickly with a smiley face.

This is me—being myself. We'll see if it works.

7:46 p.m.
Okay, so soccer tryouts weren't that bad. Basically, Emma, Aisha, and I got to kick the ball around together for an hour. We talked about what teachers we liked most (Mrs. Gridden) and the least (Mr. Robertson). We gossiped about whether two people in our history class were most definitely hooking up and whether the rumors that there's a big retro-theme party coming up this weekend are true (probably not).

For a moment, I forgot I don't like Aisha—or at least that I'm trying to tell myself that I don't like Aisha.

10:31 p.m.
My day sort of went like this: Was running late for class and ran into the wrong classroom. Dropped my lunch tray in the middle of the cafeteria. I forgot my English homework at home. Considered again whether I should try to get into that coding club. But then got an email that we all made the soccer team.

4:45 p.m.
It's our first soccer practice. The coach says it's all about having fun and getting us warmed up and ready for the season. When we take to the field, I start to think about the kids in the after-school coding club. They're probably just sitting in a boring room not even talking to each other. I'm not missing it. At all. Kind of. Okay, maybe just a little bit. But that's the thing about high school—it doesn't always feel like you can be you. Sometimes you have to be the you your friends want.

8:46 p.m.
An email pops up in my school account:

. . . .

Hi Charlie,
My name is Jack. I'm a sophomore and am the student lead for the coding club. Mr. Danson told me you had tried to register. I just wanted to let you know that it's currently full, but if a spot opens up, I'll reach out.
Jack

. . . .

Before I can lash out about how dumb, stupid, worthless, and what a waste the coding club probably is, I get a text from Emma telling me that she stayed after soccer practice to hang with a guy from the boys' varsity team—and they kissed. Not just a kiss. Her first kiss. She says his name is Nick and that he's cute. "Not Cole-Sprouse-level cute," she clarifies. "But still, cute." The suck-face session feels like a betrayal, even though I know Emma doesn't mean it that way. There are two groups in the high school hierarchy—the girls who have been kissed and the girls who haven't. And now we're divided.

I can't keep up. First I was stressing about what to wear to school and how to not be socially awkward at a soccer game, and now I have to worry about the fact that I've never even been to first base.

Who makes all of these random high school goals? And what if you're not interested in them? I guess that's what they call an outcast.

10:12 p.m.

Things I've Googled since I've learned Emma kissed a boy:
- What is the average age for a first kiss?
- Is it normal if you just started sophomore year and have never kissed someone?
- Do most people use their tongue for a first kiss?
- How do you practice kissing someone?

One website says the average age for a first kiss is 14, but another says 13. Either way, I'm behind.

Friday, September 1

3:30 p.m.

I survived my first week. It was huge having Emma's help putting together what to wear. It made life so much easier. Everyone needs a friend like Emma.

Wait—that's it!

Everyone needs a friend like Emma—or an app! Imagine how amazing it would be to have an app where you can upload all of your outfits, and it will put together fun combinations for you. You're over the striped shirt that's been sitting in your closet forever, and suddenly the app pairs it with a pair of leather pants and you're obsessed. You could plan out your whole calendar.

Not only will an idea like this make coding look cool—it will keep me looking cool to Emma.

I'm so excited. I check the app store and it doesn't look like exactly what I want exists. There are some similar ideas, but I want to make my app even better. It would allow you to upload pictures of everything in your closet so it can put together outfits for you, poll your besties about your look, as well as include a section filled with style inspiration, sort of like an "app-azine." (That's an app + a magazine. I'm making that a thing.)

6:30 p.m.

My dad is making dinner, so I decide to tell him about my app. It doesn't exist yet—the idea is only minutes old—but it seems like such a part of me, trying to hide it feels as awkward as hiding an arm. I explain everything while my dad chops veggies.

"That's a cool idea," he says, as he stirs some sauce into the stir fry. "Have you thought of a name?"

"I'm not totally sure. I'm not even sure I know how to choose a name."

"Well, it should be unique," he explains. "But it should also be something that means something to you."

"Well, it has to do with style, and I really want it to be a style app for girls like me—girls who love fashion and a lot of other things, too, like feminism," I say. I'm still trying to talk it out when my mom walks in the door.

"She's working on an app," my dad says. "Coding stuff."

"Amazing, Charlie," my mom says as she drops her stuff on the table. "This isn't going to interfere with your schoolwork is it? I know you're doing soccer, too. I just don't want you to get burned out."

"No, I'm good," I say.

"Great," she says. "Who wants to go to BAM this weekend to see a new play?"

She's already moved on, but my brain is still turning.

Wait, the name—I've got it.

The Fashionist: An app for feminist fashion lovers.

10:14 p.m.

I should be sleeping but I've never been so energized by something before. I know how to code a little bit from camp and when I taught myself using a program called Scratch, but there are so many things I don't know. *How much money do I need to code an app? Do I need to wait until I have a college degree? If not, do I need to be at least 18? How do you even begin?*

I go online to see what I can find. I discover that there are actually forums with group message boards to help newbie coders. I find one that looks cool.

I click "JOIN." That's my big mistake.

every girl deserves to take part in creating the technology that will change our world, and change who runs it

Malala Yousafzai

#TwoFaced

2:30 p.m.

All I can think about is my app idea. My very own thing. My metamorphosis. But I have to tuck my excitement away for most of the day because I have soccer. We have an extra-long practice and then a friendly match.

As I run around the field, it's my mind that's truly racing. I can't wait to share the idea with my teammates and everyone at school. Mostly, I can't wait to share it with Emma. It's hard to keep it on the DL, but there are a million reasons why she can't know yet:

1. I might not even be able to create the app.
2. I haven't fully researched the idea to know if something similar already exists.
3. She might not totally get it.
4. She might tell Aisha.
5. I want it to be perfect, so she's totally impressed.

5:04 p.m.

When I finally get home, I look into whether I can legit pull it off. My coding skills are very basic. I do a little digging around on coding sites, like code.org and codecademy.com, to see how hard it is to create something like this. The Codecademy site has stories from people who had zero experience with coding and learned how to do it just by using the info on its pages. There was even a video of a girl who didn't look much older than me explaining how she had been nervous to start coding—she just sold her tech company to YouTube. So I guess it's possible if you are brave and confident enough to try. That's one of the most awesome things about coding—you can do it even when you're a teenager.

I'm excited. But I'm also something else. It's a familiar feeling that I recognize immediately. *It's insecurity: I'm not smart enough. No one's going to be interested in my idea. I turn everything I do into a mess. The app is a dumb concept. There are a million coders who are better than me.*

But instead of letting that stop me, I push my self-doubt aside. Because it's like, what's the worst thing that can happen? That I fail? That I make a mistake? Is there anybody that has survived life without ever making a mistake? Ever?

So I'm going to do this, although I may need a little extra boost as evidenced by the last five things in my search history:

1. Where do you find confidence?
2. How can you get confidence?
3. Once you have confidence, how do you keep it?
4. How long does confidence last?
5. Are you supposed to feel confident all the time?

7:08 p.m.

Emma sends me a text asking if we can hang out tomorrow. There's a soccer game for the varsity boys and she wants to go.

I'm in.

10:01 p.m.

My parents are downstairs hosting a dinner party. My brother is at his friend's. I'm in my room on Instagram.

I follow my school, too, and oddly enough a post just popped up with a picture of the coding club. Apparently they're designing an interactive game to inspire more kids to recycle in the community. I'm bored, so I stalk everyone in the group photo. There's one girl in the group—River. The girl from homeroom.

I see on Instagram that she's a total coder. There's one photo of her with a donut in one hand as she's typing away on her computer. Other pics reveal that she goes to Hackathons and even went to a local event where the founder of Snapchat spoke. Her last post is a call to action around net neutrality. I'm envious of her in a way I've never felt before—not even of Emma and her perfect hair. She's doing what she loves and is completely unapologetic about it.

I decide I'm out—for the soccer game.

I'm feeling so inspired by River that I want to start creating the app right now. If I wait, I'm just going to start second-guessing myself again.

Now I just need to let Emma know.

10:49 p.m.

For a long time, I debate how to get out of the soccer game. But after running through multiple scenarios in my mind, I determine there's only one option: I have to lie.

I text Emma and tell her I'm sick. I even use the green-face emoji and then follow it up with the one that's puking to really drive home that I'm not well. The kind of sick where your stomach feels completely hollow. I tell her that I'll definitely make the next one. I turn my phone off, like that somehow prevents the guilty vibes I'm feeling from transmitting through the phone. But I last only a second before I turn it back on to see her response.

Nothing.

But there is a new photo up on Instagram of Emma. It's a selfie and the caption talks about how she's going to the soccer game tomorrow. She tagged Aisha. I actually feel sick for real. The kind of sick where your stomach feels completely hollow.

Sunday, September 3

10:09 a.m.

I wake up feeling a little better. It can be frustrating that so many feelings can live in my body at the same time: self-doubt, anxiety, confidence, passion, happiness, confusion. But I realize that's just part of life. I take a screenshot of my favorite inspirational quote from Emily Weiss of Glossier: "That power of the individual person—just the girl—is infinite." See, I can be anything, I can do everything, I have girl boss power. Sometimes you just need to give yourself a pep talk.

It kind of works. I feel strangely focused. I start sketching photos of what my app could look like. (After doing some more reading on the coding sites, this seems to be the thing you do first.) I make a little progress, but there are so many different ways to do things. Millions. Maybe billions. There are quite a few things I need to figure out before I can make true progress. I need to know what kind of operating system I'm going to develop this for—that will determine if it works on an iPhone or an Android. I also need to figure out how to make sure it works just as well on a tablet as it does on a phone and even what coding language to choose.

I need a little break to think over some of these options. I click on an episode of *Riverdale*. I've already binged the season, but this will help me clear my mind. I plop down onto my bed and refresh my feed out of habit.

There it is—a bunch of photos of Emma and Aisha at the soccer game together.

I shouldn't care. I bailed on them.

But I do.

"That power of the individual person—just the girl—is infinite."

My phone buzzes.

My stomach sinks.

Will it be another post of Emma and Aisha having so much fun together? Or a text from Emma telling me that she knows I wasn't sick today?

It's neither.

It's a private message from someone with the username Seven.

SEVEN: Hey what's up? You still need help?

Huh? I have no clue who this person is and I definitely don't know what I need help with. Whoever it is must have the wrong person.

ME: I think you're looking for someone else. Don't need any help.

SEVEN: Gotcha. No prob. I was in the coding chat and thought you had a question about something. I must have clicked on the wrong username.

Oh, that's right. When I joined that coding forum the other night, I did put a few questions on the message board. I had actually forgotten about it. Given that I have only more questions now, maybe this Seven can help me figure out how to even begin creating an app.

ME: Oh, sorry. I forgot about that. I have an app idea and I'm trying to figure out the best way to get started. I don't have much experience. I don't even know if I should have been in that coding forum.

SEVEN: Of course you should. That's what it's there for. ☺

A smiley.

ME: True!

SEVEN: Still stuck?

ME: Yeah. I might be even more stuck.

SEVEN: I would start by choosing what coding language you want to develop in and then brush up on that. If you learn how to teach your computer to do tricks—just like a dog—you can make it do anything. But instead of sit, fetch, or come here, you make the computer do things like bold letters, make a photo square, link to this page, or turn this green.

ME: You make it sound so simple. But I'm majorly struggling.

SEVEN: Got anything I could see? If I had specifics, I could give you a little better guidance. "Study your coding" probably sounds like pretty lame advice. I've got better. ;)

A wink.

ME: Yeah, I sketched out a few things. Where should I send?

SEVEN: You can upload the doc here.

I attach it to the chat screen and hit send. A few minutes pass.

SEVEN: This is a really great idea. For just getting started, you're wicked smart. Why don't you try fiddling around with some code and send me the beginnings of what you have in a week or so? And I can definitely give you advice about operating systems and device compatibility and all that stuff.

I don't know why, but I immediately trust Seven. Maybe it's because he called me smart. Maybe it's because he seemed to view me in a way that most people don't immediately see. Maybe it's because it felt like he was flirting with me, and no one ever had before. I don't know. Anyway, it is great to have somebody to ask questions to, but for the most part I want to figure out everything myself. I think that is part of the fun of the coding—playing around and seeing where it takes you.

I waste no time and start practicing on code.org. It comes surprisingly easy to me.

2:39 p.m.

Just over two hours later, and I've already designed and created the lilac diamond I want to be the app's logo and what will show up when you search for it in the app store. I'm happy for the long Labor Day weekend so I can work on this for another day. I'm thinking about a lot of things—what functions to add, how to make links work, if I should charge for the app.

8:44 a.m.

I'm back at school after a long weekend. Emma, Aisha, and I sit together in homeroom. The two of them are talking about the soccer game. They are telling stories about all the hot guys who hit on them, the party invites they scored, and how they're going to do it again next weekend.

"I was so sick I had to go to the emergency room," I say.

I blurt it out before I even realize what I'm saying. I know that I'm lying, and as soon as I say it, the thing I feel most is regret. The whole moment seems like it happened in slow motion—the frozen looks on both Emma's and Aisha's faces, the sudden silence of everyone around us—and yet, at the same time, it seems like it happened so quickly the words fell out of my mouth. There is an unexpected redness that creeps up from my chest to my cheeks. It's hotter than blushing, and brighter. It almost burns. But nothing sears and hurts more than Emma first, and then Aisha, saying that they're glad I'm feeling better and then continuing the gossipy chat about their weekend.

Replaced.

Control + alt + delete our friendship. I don't need to be an expert coder to see that's what's happening.

Just as my tears are about to flow, I bite my lip to keep them from falling. I refuse to let them out and force them back inside through sheer anger. I tell myself that I deserve this after lying to my best friend, even though deep down I know I want to tell her the truth. I want to share my app idea with her—but just not yet. Despite my best efforts, the tears that feel like hot jelly are back.

I need to stop thinking—about this, anyway. So I look down at my phone and start researching different fashion apps, like Stitch Fix, Stylect, and FAD, to see what other style geniuses are doing. I make mental notes of all the things I like:

- Ability to shop your friend's closet
- Ways for users to upload their outfits for others to see
- A search bar
- An option to log in using your social media accounts

The bell rings, and my tears disappear. Aisha and Emma disappear through the halls, too.

6:03 p.m.

I retreat to my room to work on the app. I've been a lousy friend lately, but coding gives me a sense of comfort. I guess because I feel the most confident when I'm coding—it's something I'm actually pretty good at. I see a few people I know from coding forums are online and send them each a message. Seven responds first.

Me: Hi!

Seven: Hey there, CharlieGirl.

It's my username, so I know he's not saying it to be cute. But it's cute.

Me: I've done some coding and will def have some stuff to show you soon.

Seven: Awesome.

Me: Yea, I've narrowed down my big ideas.

Seven: Tell me more.

For the next 63 minutes I talk with Seven. He asks me a ton of different questions: What did I envision the home screen to look like? Would I want outfits to also include accessories? What did I think were good search options? How would I incorporate social media so everyone could share their looks? Brainstorming together makes me think about things I've not considered before. We speak the same language. After all, we are coders.

10:11 p.m.

Me: U there?

Seven: Always for you.

Me: I was going over it, and I think girls need to be able to follow other girls with styles they like, too. It's kind of like you have your own feed of fashion inspo on the app. But do you think that sounds redundant, since people already follow fashion influencers on social media? I'm thinking this helps put all of your fashion in one place.

Seven: Good idea. You should get to bed, pretty girl.

He thinks I'm smart *and* pretty. I'm blushing to the point it feels like my cheeks are pulsing—like a heartbeat. But I leave out the emoji that shows that.

7:46 p.m.

So happy to be back from soccer practice. When I was on the field, the sun was setting, leaving one side of the sky darker than the other. If you looked to the left, there were streaks of cotton-candy pink light so vivid I could almost taste it. But to the right, it was so muted it looked like someone had tried to erase the color. How can one thing look so different? But then again, that's exactly what my life feels like right now. I have school and soccer and studying. But then I have my app and Seven. I wonder if Seven would mind telling me where he's from. Or even how old he is. Is it weird that I don't know those things?

1:30 p.m.

I just finished my math test and think I did pretty well, especially since I didn't really study. There's only one other person who finished faster than me—River. My grades can't start dropping or I will lose my computer or phone. My mom is a fanatic about grades.

My plan was to practice my equations last night, but I ended up messaging with Seven until late. He had a bunch more questions about my app. Pretty much everything he tells me I already know, but it's nice to have someone to bounce ideas off of. He didn't get to answer where he was from because his

Internet was being spotty, but he did tell me he's 17.

River and I both end up leaving class at the same time, but she never once looks my way. She's typing like crazy on her phone and then stops off at her locker to grab her laptop before disappearing around the corner. I want to find a way to tell her that I'm into coding, too. But she never came back and I had to get to next period.

2:00 p.m.

I decide to do a little more digging on River. For two reasons: My English literature class is majorly boring, and I really want to connect with another girl who's into computers like me.

I've already checked out her feed once or twice—or 27 times—but after clicking around on some of the other coding club members' accounts, I see she has a Twitter account. She's retweeted out a bunch of links to a local skateboard store.

Hobby?

A little more clicking, and no. At least not a skateboarding hobby—but maybe a coding hobby. She created an app for the store. I know because there's an About section on their website and it talks about River and the app—it not only allows you to shop the store but also to create cool videos and upload them to the community page.

She's an app developer.

Like me.

I decide to get up the courage to ask her about it. I even create an elaborate story about how I was shopping for my skateboarding brother when by chance I saw the app she created on the store's website. She definitely couldn't know the truth.

But as soon as I get to her locker, she seems flustered. She ends up asking me if I'll cover for her since she needs to take care of something that went wrong with her app. She wants me to tell the teacher that she's sick.

"Sure," I say. And for a second I even feel good about it. She brought up the app, so I won't have to make up a fake story when I ask her about it later. But I realize I still have to lie. Again. It's an uncomfortable feeling that pinballs around my body and leaves me feeling like I've been carved into something new—a liar. It is that uncomfortable. It is exactly how I felt when I told Emma

I had gone to the emergency room.

Anyway, I tell the teacher that River is sick. I feel less red this time but just as guilty.

7:23 p.m.

I download River's app to see what it's all about, and I can't believe how insanely well she built this thing. It almost makes *me* want to be a skater chick. The technology she used to allow people to upload videos and photos is exactly what I need to figure out how to do in my app so people can upload photos of their outfits. I've been practicing my coding and am getting better and better. I've even got some pieces of the app done. But on this part, I'm struggling. I don't know how to display horizontal photos properly or how to change the size of them so they fit on the screen. I told Seven about it, but he's been quiet the last few days. River killed it. Maybe she could help me figure it out?

Friday, September 8

11:30 a.m.

I know that River has a history class at this time, so I position myself sort of near where I think she would walk. Just as she's coming by, I drop my notebook and by the time I bend down to pick it up she's gone. Fail.

8:30 p.m.

No big tests to study for. No soccer practice tonight. Hello, weekend!

Emma includes me on a big group text. Apparently there's a big party tonight, and she invited a bunch of people to meet up with her there. I respond that I miss her—I do!—but I can't make it out tonight. She sends back a broken-heart emoji. I almost have a change of heart but there's too much work to be done on the app, and the weekend is prime time to get it done.

And even better: Seven is online. I send him my latest code. I figured out something major recently, and I know he'll appreciate that I totally nailed it.

SEVEN: I think before you try to do too much, you should start teaching yourself some more.

ME: Like what?

SEVEN: Like Swift. It's another one of those computer languages that iOS happens to use. It's Apple's operating system and it would be good for you to know. There's an online course from Stanford University that shows you how to build apps in this language, and Apple has a free e-book on their website. Plus, you should probably brush up on HTML, JavaScript, and Python.

My heart sinks. I'm happy to have Seven's input but for the first time it seems like he's doubting me, and that he doesn't think I'm ready or that I have what it takes to develop an app. He isn't being flirty or funny. But before I can spiral into a full meltdown over my keyboard, this:

SEVEN: You are honestly one of the best coders I know who has been coding for only such a short time. Legit. I just want you to learn as much as you can so your app is as good as it can be. What happens if you need to hire some coders? You'll need to have an understanding of a few languages.

I feel like we're clicking. Not just computer keys. But really clicking. The way I've heard it's supposed to happen when you're into someone. It crosses my mind that I don't really know Seven and that meeting IRL seems impossible at this point. But how well do I really know anyone? Just because I could tell you what classes and hair color the guys at my school have, so what? Is that knowing someone? I know that Seven is selfless, thoughtful, and smart. And for now, that's enough.

11:49 p.m.

Seven had to go, but I stay up late to work on Swift. I'm slaying it. It's actually pretty logical. Something I can't really say about my Spanish class or my relationship with Emma.

```
1. let skirts = 3
2. let shirts = 5
3. let skirtsSummary = "I have \ (skirts)  skirts."
4. let outfitSummary = "I have \ (skirts + shirts)  outfits."
```

I've been making such serious progress that I decide it's time to officially start programming my app, so I download Xcode. It's like a little digital notebook to write your code in. I start adding in the small lines of code that I've toyed with that will eventually create my app. The first line of code that Seven told me all official programmers create is to make their computer say, "Hello world."

I try it out, and there is it on my screen. Programmed by me.

```
println ("Good night, world")
```

Saturday, September 9

11:30 a.m.

Tired. Exhausted. Sleepy. I had an early soccer game today and could barely tie my cleats after being up so late, let alone run around a giant grassy field.

After the game, it never crosses my mind that Emma may want to hang. I've been so distracted trying to make progress on my app—but she invites me to go and grab a matcha with her.

"I don't think I can," I say. It feels like I have to push the words out of my mouth. All I want to do is hang with Emma.

"Why not?"

"I have a lot of homework to catch up on," I say.

"Really? Our teachers didn't give us much." She says this in a way that feels like she doesn't believe me.

"Sucks for me. Let's plan something later."

Emma mentions that we should study together later this week, and then we both leave the field. Watching Emma walk away alone makes me feel guilty, but I try to justify how I'm acting. I tell myself the only reason Emma wants to spend time with me is because Aisha is at her dad's house this weekend. But I don't truly believe it. It's harder to lie to yourself.

9:13 p.m.

I see on Snapchat that Emma walked to Ample Hills Creamery with Aisha (okay, so she isn't at her dad's) at the same time that Seven sends me a message that a girl like me shouldn't be at home on a Saturday night. "No coding tonight," he says. It causes an anxiety in my stomach that swishes around and makes me feel queasy.

Seven is probably right. I should have gone to hang out with Emma. I miss her. I've been such a crappy friend. Even if I want to wait to show her my app, that doesn't mean I have to go MIA. I send her a text.

ME: I saw your story and that pic of you in that embroidered jacket. You looked amazing. Sorry I missed!

EMMA: Thanks, babe! Come with next time! I really miss you.
I feel like our friendship is back on track in three lines.

Sunday, September 10

10:14 a.m.

I barely avoid a huge problem.

My dad walks into my room wearing a pair of sweatpants and holding a steaming cup of coffee. He says I've been studying a lot and spending too much time on the computer. He wants to talk to my teacher about my workload. I tell him things will ease up soon, and he seems to buy it.

If it's not friend drama, it's my family.

3:55 p.m.

The first screen of my app is complete. I'm pretty proud of myself because it wasn't easy getting to this point. I had been going back and forth about how to do it for a while. Even though my coding has gotten so much stronger, there were still so many decisions to make that impacted everything. I had to decide if I wanted to build my app for the iPhone or for a Samsung or Windows. So. Much. Technical. Stuff.

But I did a little digging and eventually figured it out. There are different stores that sell apps: the Apple App Store, Google Play, and Microsoft's Windows App. All three places use their own operating system. So, for example, apps from the App Store are downloaded with iPhones. And the same is true with Google Play apps and Windows apps—they only work with Androids or Windows operating systems, like Samsungs and Nokias.

There is a computer language that all these systems understand, so it is possible to create something that would work for all three, which seemed like the best plan to me. But then I discovered that the apps aren't sold in all the shops and are more like websites.

Next, I decided that—even though Apple has strict guidelines and requires more time because you have to go through a selection process before going live, and Android hardly checks the apps at all—I would develop my app to work with iPhones. After all, that is the phone all my friends and I have.

See? So. Much. Technical. Stuff. But to be honest, it's pretty thrilling.

8:47 a.m.

I'm *this close* to just telling everyone everything.

Emma is wearing the same embroidered jacket to school that I complimented her on over the weekend, and I want to fill her in on The Fashionist so badly. I want to tell her how she was the one who inspired it. On top of that, my dad saw the glow of my computer screen underneath my bedroom door last night and burst in and made me put my computer away. He was mad—at me, at my teacher, at school. I'm not sure. But I almost told him what I was working on so he would understand this is all temporary.

But I held it in. Right now, it's just the secret that Seven and I share.

1:31 p.m.

Something amazing happened. River and I are paired up for a project in math class. I decide to finally bring up my app.

"You mentioned the other day that you have an app. I'm working on one, too." As I say it, I wait for her eyes to light up and connect with mine but that never happened. She kind of mumbled something about how that was cool and then kept writing in her notebook.

"Would you like to see it?" I don't wait to see what she says. I open my phone and pull up the early pieces of what I've been working on. She takes the phone and swipes around a few times.

"Nice," she says.

"I'm still working on it and need a little help. I taught myself to code, so I'm not super great yet." I hope by adding that last sentence, it gives me a little cred.

"Yeah, there are a few rookie things wrong here," she says. "The resolution of your photos is too low and the way you've coded your header is all wrong. If you ever need help, DM me."

I feel the buzz of my phone on the desk. I glance quickly and see a text.

Emma: Everything ok? I've been trying to give you space because it seems like you're juggling a lot of homework and stuff. But I'd love if we could find some time to hang out.

I want to answer. But I'm preoccupied.

Why didn't Seven tell me about these mistakes?

7:00 p.m.

I'm deep into research trying to figure out how to fix some of the issues that River brought up, when another problem pops up—this time in the form of a text message from Emma.

EMMA: Uh, thanks for the response earlier.

Shoot. It suddenly hits me that I didn't get back to her.

EMMA: Also, you broke our Snap streak! We had that going for over six months.

Double shoot. Total fail on my part there, too. I try to think of a good response—something that shows how bad I feel and that doesn't require me to lie about why I've been MIA. Nothing seems right, so I settle on the obvious.

ME: Sorry.

I don't hear anything back.

Wednesday, September 13

5:01 p.m.

I can't avoid the situation with Emma forever. We're at soccer practice together. She looks perfect—as always—in bike shorts and a graphic sweatshirt. Where does she even find this stuff?

She darts around me with the ball, while I try to dart around the truth while also trying to explain everything to her. I try to come up with all sorts of convincing reasons why I've been so flaky. I say my parents are contemplating making me get a job, that I have so much homework lately I don't even have time to sleep, and that my mom has been sick with a weird flu so I've been helping out more around the apartment. She doesn't say much, and maybe that says everything.

5:59 p.m.

Until 58 minutes later, when she does have something to say.

EMMA: I'm still really confused why you just dropped off the face of the planet. I'm sure you at least have time to text me.

And then in a classic Emma move, another text follows in quick succession.

EMMA: I knew sophomore year was going to change you.

But that's just the thing. I thought I was supposed to change. Isn't that what Emma was doing when she was shopping for the perfect first-day outfit? My change was just different.

I don't respond at first because I don't know what to say—or more like, I can't say what I want to. Not yet. I decide to play it safe.

ME: I'll make it up to you. Promise.

I take a selfie, put a filter on it that has a bunch of pink hearts floating around my face, and send it to Emma on Snapchat—the start of a new streak.

7:47 p.m.

I decide to DM River and ask her questions on some of the fixes I'm having a problem with—12 questions, actually. There were 13 but I took off "Do you know a coder named Seven?"

I need to get the app done so I can come clean with Emma about what I've been doing with my time. Our friendship is hanging by a thread. And it's all my fault. I just want it to be the most amazing thing ever before I show her—I want it to be impressive.

Thursday, September 14

6:59 a.m.

I wake up to a message from Seven. He explains that he's been so swamped with a project and that he's sorry he's been kind of quiet. He quickly addresses why he didn't fix all of the problems with my app:

SEVEN: I want you to learn, k? I knew you would figure it out. You're smart, babe!

No guy had ever called me *babe* before. It feels like we're getting serious, and in other ways it feels like things are exactly the same. I still don't even know where Seven lives, not even the country. But he calls me *babe*. I tell myself that online relationships are different.

9:15 a.m.

River shows up to school with all of the answers to my fixes. I suddenly feel guilty for asking her. I should have tried to figure them out for myself, like Seven said. If I was a serious programmer, I shouldn't rely on River to do everything for me.

I decide to mention the forum to her. She knows of it and says there are some cool people on there, but also some strange ones.

"Do you think I should change my name? It's CharlieGirl." I almost say it on purpose, so that maybe she'll track me down on the forum and we can talk about coding even more.

"No one cares what your forum name is, Charlie." She pauses. "Girl."

12:46 p.m.
Emma and I haven't really talked much since she sent me that last text message, but I see her in the hallway and ask her if she wants to walk to a nearby deli for lunch. Aisha was there, so I include her, too. Emma agrees, so—progress?

2:01 p.m.
English literature is boring. Really boring.

Friday, September 15

6:41 p.m.
The weekend's here and it's prime coding time. I take Seven's advice and I am determined to get better on my own. I search some sites and find the most useful list:
- Code = programming rules or a programming language—the language computers understand
- Developer = someone who develops software
- Bug = a fault in programming language, like a spelling mistake

Did I just call this list useful? I'm such a nerd.

Before I keep reading, my phone lights up. Every buzz, beep, and beam of light makes me feel fluttery because I know it could be Seven. This time it's a text from Emma, asking me if I want to go over to her apartment and watch Netflix.

ME: I can't hang tonight because I'm finishing up my app. I can tell you more about it later, but I want you to know it's inspired by you.

I didn't actually send that. I had it all typed out but then I deleted it.

ME: My mom grounded me because I got into a huge fight with my brother. She is the worst.

That I actually did send. Digital lies are the easiest. I follow it up with a truth.

ME: I want to chill with you, tho. Next weekend?

EMMA: Yah.

4:02 p.m.

Programming day success!

```
1.var favoriteList:  [String]  =  ["Skirt black 3", "Bag Prada 2"]
2.//  favoriteList has been initialized with two initial items
```

```
1.favoriteList +=  ["top 2"]
2.//  favoriteList now contains 3 items
3.favoriteList +=  ["headband 4", "tie 1", "knee socks 7"]
4.// favoriteList now contains 6 items
```

```
1.  class SurveyQuestion {
2.          var text: String
3.          var response: String?
4.          init(text: String) {
5.              self.text = text
6.          }
7.          func ask() {
8.              println (text)
9.          }
10. }
11. let fashionQuestion = SurveyQuestion(text: "Do you like the
    preppy look?")
12. fashionQuestion.ask()
13. // prints "Do you like the preppy look?"
14. fashionQuestion.response = "I heart the preppy look."
```

Sunday, September 17

9:13 a.m.

I just know my mom is going to make us all spend the day together, so I get up extra early to finish up a few more things on the app. It's getting really close to being in a good place.

Wait, nothing is running like it should and all of my tests are crashing in my prototype. I could text River, but I decide to lean on my rock—Seven.

I didn't hear back from Seven right away, so I send him seven more messages—appropriately. I also text River.

9:19 a.m.

I start to wonder where Seven lives. Does he live somewhere that he can't answer my messages because he's asleep? Maybe he's in a time zone on the other side of the country. How little I know about him suddenly makes me uneasy, but I push it out of my mind. I know everything about River, and she isn't responding to me, either.

9:23 a.m.

Why can't River just respond?

9:24 a.m.

Why can't Seven just respond?

9:28 a.m.

Seven *can* respond—and he does.

SEVEN: Hey Charlie! I'm actually traveling right now. It could be an unhandled exception. You probably did something that doesn't work on all sites, so you'll need to switch up the code. I can help you on Monday. K?

My rock.

11:10 a.m.

Just like I expected, my parents are making me join them at the movies this afternoon. My dad is back on his speech about how it's not healthy to be locked in your room all day with a phone and a computer. Instead of hopping on the train or jumping in a taxi, we walk together through the park for "fresh air" according to my dad's grand plan. I should be mad, but I'm actually looking forward to getting out for a bit.

Plus, I'm still buzzing that Seven took time out of his busy schedule to get back to me. I'm starting to wonder what exactly a relationship is and how you know when one begins.

12:15 p.m.

The theater is packed. There are three seats left in row 18 and one in row 19, so I offer to sit by myself. The movie is totally boring. But hello, there's Wi-Fi!

I log on to the forum to see if I can figure this out before Seven gets back to me on Monday. I want to show him that I am becoming a master. After a few messages, no one really thinks it's an unhandled exception. I feel frustrated that I can't figure out this problem, but also pretty good that at least I'm not the only one who doesn't get it.

12:33 p.m.

River finally gets back to me and says she isn't sure how to fix it, either. She can help me tomorrow, but I don't really feel like waiting. I'd rather get to the bottom of this myself.

The guy sitting next to me is getting annoyed about the light from my screen. I tuck my phone into my pocket. I guess I'll have to wait.

8:13 p.m.

I keep going through the forum and finally figure out what's wrong. There's an issue with my code. I know what it is, I think. There's something called an infinite loop, which apparently is a common beginner's mistake. In fact, the address for the previous headquarters of Apple in San Francisco was named for this mistake: 1 Infinite Loop (at least their new address is not making fun of coders;-). Everything keeps crashing because I never changed the code from *newFavorites* to *totalAmountFavorites*. This is what it should look like:

```
1. let newFavorites = 0
2. while newFavorites < totalNumberFavorites {
3.     // add clothing item
4.     totalNumberFavorites += 1
5. }
```

It feels pretty amazing to figure it out and fix it all on my own. I'm getting really good at this whole coding thing. I didn't even need any help from Seven or River. I've been feeling so many things—excitement, frustration, guilt, love maybe?—but in this moment, for once, it feels like I'm good at something.

9:11 p.m.

I know Seven is traveling but I decide to message him and tell him that I got everything figured out. And then I keep coding.

Monday, September 18

1:14 a.m.

Not really awake, but I'm pretty sure a message from Seven came in.

: SEVEN: I thought we were going to fix this together.
  He seems mad. Am I dreaming?

7:01 a.m.

Nope, not a dream. It was a message from Seven, and he definitely seems annoyed with me.

10:20 a.m.

I'm in history class but I'm not really here, at least not mentally. I can't understand why Seven would be so upset with me. Didn't he want me to take initiative and do things on my own? I'm also surprised by how much those few words hurt. They were like pointed arrows that popped the air out of whatever good feelings I was having.

Everyone around me is exchanging stories about their weekend. From the new clothes they got to details of Cole's house party—Cole is a popular kid with a lot of upperclassmen friends, maybe even Finn—to Friday night football game gossip.

Out of nowhere, Aisha turns to me and asks what I did. It's nice to feel included.

"Just homework," I say. And then, remembering the excuse I gave Emma about why I couldn't see her, "because I was grounded."

8:46 p.m.

I'm putting all of my focus into finishing up The Fashionist. I can't wait to show it to Emma.

But first, I message Seven to tell him that we should really talk, or in our case, chat. I'm sure I'll wake up to a message from him that calls me babe and tells me that he's sorry. I bet he even suggests we try to Skype or FaceTime or even meet up in person if we live close enough. He's been asking me so many questions about my app lately, sometimes I just feel like it's his nerves disguising what he truly wants to say.

Thursday, September 21

10:10 p.m.

The bad news: I still haven't heard from Seven.

The good news: I decide it doesn't make any sense to keep the app from Emma. The plan has always been to show it to her in some big, bright reveal. But all the amazing things I'm doing with the app sort of mean nothing, since I have to constantly lie and miss out on time with my best friend. The Fashionist may not be entirely done, but it's in a good enough place that I'm going to tell her everything.

Friday, September 22

8:34 a.m.

I'm the very first person in homeroom because I want to talk to Emma first thing. I want to invite her over this weekend to show her The Fashionist. She walks in just a few minutes later—but she's with Aisha. Instead of changing my plans, I decide to invite them both. I'm so proud of the app, I'm not embarrassed to be a coder anymore. So if Aisha knows who I *really* am, it's no big deal.

Emma thinks that something is up and keeps trying to guess. "Did you give your room a giant makeover? Did you get a dog? Are you moving?" She did not guess: You've been creating a fashion app.

2:44 p.m.
I'm supposed to be making a Picasso-like drawing right now. But all I can think about is showing Emma the app tomorrow. Is she going to love it? Hate it? I decide on the former—or maybe the latter.

9:00 p.m.
I clean up my room and try to come up with what I'm going to say to Emma and Aisha. I suck at speaking in front of people. Last year in speech class, I got a C-. My teacher gave me a list of ways I could improve:
- Make more eye contact with your audience
- Speak slower
- Don't mumble so much
- Speak louder

But none of it really explains how to tell your best friend that you've been lying to her for weeks. Maybe that part will be okay to mumble over?

9:10 p.m.
I'm about to carry all the dirty dishes out of my room when I see a text from Emma. Oh shoot, she's going to cancel.

EMMA: I know I'll see you tomorrow, but I just want to make sure everything's OK?
ME: Yeah. Why wouldn't it be?
EMMA: Well, you're just calling this meeting thing and I know it's not your style. I feel like something must be wrong, like your parents are getting divorced or your mom is sick. It seems like that would be why you've been so distant.

A knot forms in my stomach and it feels like it will never come undone. That's because I know Emma mentions my mom being sick because of the lie I told her.

ME: I actually have good news to tell you.

And then I pull an Emma and send another message just a few seconds later.

ME: But seriously, Em, thank you for checking. You ARE the best BFF.
EMMA: OK, but give me a hint now. You know how impatient I am! You have a

secret boyfriend?

Me: Ha. No. Better. It will be worth the wait.

All of the feel-good stuff with Emma makes me wonder about Seven. I miss him, too. I should have made more of an effort to get in touch with him. I can see why his feelings were hurt. I can fix this.

I tap out an apology and click send.

User not found. What??

code is a superpower every young woman should be able to access

Karlie Kloss

#Charmer

3

7:45 a.m.

Once again it's the weekend and I should be sleeping in, but I'm wide awake. I can't wait to show The Fashionist to Emma and Aisha. I especially want to tell Emma about the "app-azine" part of my idea. I'm going to pitch the idea for her to work on that section. Flattery as my apology. But as the moment to tell Emma the truth looms closer, my belief that the app is going to not only fix girls' wardrobe problems but also my friendship with Emma seems to get further away. I've been kind of a crappy person and I can't even fully explain to myself why I've been acting this way.

8:30 a.m.

Parents are weird.

Sometimes I feel so annoyed by my mom, but when I go into the kitchen this morning she offers to pick up some pizza and snacks for when Emma and Aisha come over later. Best mom ever. And she already bought rainbow bagels for breakfast. It's not even 9 a.m., and my Insta is already on point.

1:03 p.m.

I know Emma and Aisha have arrived before I even see them.

"Oh yes, rainbow bagels," Emma squeals. My mom had let my friends in and they saw the leftover bagels. I'm glad to see they both are loving the doughy circles of goodness—a multicolored olive branch.

I don't know if there's a right time to begin, so I just go for it. "I invited you both here because I want to show you something," I say as I pull out my laptop.

"Is this some sort of presentation?" Emma asks, seemingly impressed.

"Sort of—but better," I explain. I pull up the first slide. It says The Fashionist in giant gold letters that almost sparkle and shimmer like sequins. (I've also gotten very good at Photoshop.)

Emma and Aisha still aren't saying much. It might be because their mouths are stuffed with bagels.

"When I started sophomore year, I could not figure out what to wear. I had new clothes but also old stuff, and I just completely lacked the skill to put it all together. Emma, I was so amazed at how you looked at my random piles of clothes and created all of those incredible outfits for me. I thought to myself, 'What if everyone had an Emma?' And then I realized that they could. For the past few weeks, I have been working on an app that is basically like a personal stylist in your pocket. It allows you to upload everything in your closet to the app, and it will come up with looks for you. Right now that's all it does, but I want it to be even better. I have all sort of ideas, but one of the ideas I'm most excited about is the 'app-azine' feature. It's an editorial part of the app where we highlight fashion influencers and give style advice to our readers. The app will also be able to make suggestions on things to buy if you want to switch up your look."

My plan was to stop there. But then the truth comes out.

"I have been doing this alone and keeping it a secret for a couple of reasons. I guess a part of me has been insecure about it. I felt like if the only thing I had to show was an idea, it wouldn't look very impressive and would just be lame. Saying that I'm building an app is like declaring as a high school freshman that I'm going to Harvard. It's like, okay, sure you are. But I wasn't just insecure about the app. I was insecure about our friendship, too, Emma. You're popular, and I'm not. I felt like the moment you realized that, our friendship would be over. I thought creating this app might finally put me on your level. But as I've been building the app, I realized that my plan was backfiring, because it seemed like I was always lying to you or declining a chance to hang out. That's when I realized that I didn't want to create an app for you—I want to create it *with* you."

My voice almost didn't sound like my own I was so nervous. The only thing that sounded worse was the silence. I clicked through the rest of the slides to show them what the app actually looks like, but my computer kept freezing and at one point I had to shut everything down and start over.

Rookie.

Once it started back up, I realize the clothing combinations I put in the slides feel less *Teen Vogue* and more like sloppy leggings gone rogue. Not exactly the wow factor I was going for.

"You've been lying to me?" It's a question, but when Emma says it the words sound more like a statement.

"Well...," but that's all I can get out before Emma keeps going.

"That kind of hurts, Charlie. I mean, this app is absolutely amazing. I'm so proud of you for doing something so huge—you literally just created something out of nothing. But I wish you wouldn't have shut me out of this. It really bums me out."

I feel so guilty. A giant egg forms in the back of my throat.

If I expect Aisha to snottily scoop Emma up and say that they are leaving, like some kind of friend fairy godmother, I am wrong.

"This is really cool, Charlie," Aisha says. "I think Emma is upset because she's really been missing you. But seriously, I can't believe you made all of this yourself."

Just like that, Aisha rewrites everything I've been taught about the friendship code. I've always sort of been programmed to believe that you can only have one true friend, and that girls will try to steal her from you. But the truth is, you can have a group of girls who are there for you. I see that Aisha truly wants my friendship with Emma to be repaired. She doesn't want to steal Emma from me—she wants to share her.

She continues to try and lighten the mood. "Watch out, Mark Zuckerberg—Charlie is coming for you," she jokes.

And then, for the next 15 minutes Emma lets out what I'd never given her a chance to say for the past month. She had kissed a guy and then he went and wrote terrible things about her on social media. Her older sister went off to college, and Emma was struggling with not having her home anymore. She bombed her chemistry test and missed the PSAT deadline. And through it all, she felt like she was losing her best friend—the person she would normally talk to about all of this stuff.

"I've just really been missing you," she says.

I nod, worried that the familiarity of my voice might remind her whom she's talking to again—the (former?) best friend who abandoned her.

She then switches back to the app.

"But putting all of that aside, I'm kind of speechless," Emma says. "I mean, you created an app inspired by me? This is so freaking cool. No one has ever done anything like that for me before. That in itself is pretty awesome, but the app itself is even more awesome. I mean, seriously, who just creates a personal stylist for the whole world? Apparently my best friend does!"

Emma giggles and smiles.

"But I'm not really into computers, so I don't know how I could be of help," she says. I recognize the lack of comfort—it's the same way I feel around fashion.

I explain that computers and coding and tech don't mean you are sitting around on a computer all day. I tell her that I will be doing the majority of the coding work and that she can be in charge of putting together the styling and inspiration pages.

Aisha chimes in that she's good at photography and art direction, so I extend the offer for her to help out with The Fashionist, too.

"You would be a fashion stylist for an app," I say to Emma. "Sure, I'm building an app, which feels very techie, but there are many roles to make it successful. It would be just like working for *Vogue* or *Glamour* or Song of Style—but for our own company. It's like we'd be creating a new style icon. Just imagine, Millie Bobby Brown or Kendall Jenner could follow us for fashion advice."

Sure, it sounds like I'm trying to build a company, but I'm trying to rebuild a friendship.

Our conversation is broken up when my mom pops in with pizza. As Aisha grabs a slice of pie, she asks me so many questions: "When did you start? Where did you learn to do this? Is it hard to code? What is the next step?"

The next step is for Emma to forgive me. I hope.

I don't know why it suddenly hits me, but it does. I realize it's not the app that's going to fix my friendship. It's a genuine apology.

"I'm sorry, Emma," I say. "I have been terrible. I suck at friendship sometimes and made some serious mistakes. I didn't do a good job handling all of this. I know this app is going to be fire, and it will be even better if we work on it together. I want it to be our thing, but more than anything, I just want us to be best friends again." It's not premeditated, calculated, or for show—it's real. It's that simple and Emma turns and gives me a huge squeeze.

It's the moment I know that we're truly back to being BFFs, and it's the moment we officially become a team on this app-making mission. We are The Fashionists.

Emma admits she loves the idea of creating an app-based fashion magazine to go along with my outfit combination tool, and she can't wait to get started.

Her first order of business is to create a group text for us with our team name—nothing like a giant text stream to make you feel like a legit company. "Should I invite anyone else?" She stops typing and looks up at me.

"Maybe we can invite River," I say. I explain the whole saga of how I tried to sign up for the coding club but the club was full, so I started stalking everyone in the group and then I came across the sole girl in the club, River. It sounds so ridiculous to say it out loud. We all laugh, and Emma says she'll add River if I give her the phone number.

"I am still so shook that you created an app that people can actually use—that is so huge," Aisha says.

I explain how I taught myself to code by taking online lessons and reaching out for help in coding forums.

"River has been a huge help, too," I say. "And if you girls want to learn to code a little bit, I can show you the sites I used. It's actually pretty easy, and you can use code for so many things—it's like having a little added superpower."

10:03 p.m.

I'm in bed but I feel like I'm floating.

Emma and Aisha are super involved in the app. Our group text already has over 100 messages.

Emma: Hey fam! We should partner up with fashion influencers. Maybe one day a week they can do exclusive outfit reveals on our site.

Aisha: Who's up for meeting an hour earlier tomorrow so we can figure it out?

Emma: Or two hours?

Me: Works for me.

Emma: Let's meet at my place.

Aisha is bringing her dad's tripod so we can shoot some new outfits for content. The Fashionists are on fire.

Sunday, September 24

11:29 a.m.

I show up at Emma's house for us to get started. Aisha pops in a few minutes later with a copy of *Girlboss* and breakfast from Hugo.

We start hanging up t-shirts, dresses, skirts, and everything else for us to create inspiration posts. Emma did research all night on Instagram, Pinterest, Style.com, ASOS, and a million other fashion sites. Her bedroom door looks like a vision board. We stop to take a selfie in front of it to capture our first day of work. I can't believe I'm building a business with my friends.

We decide to come up with a list of categories that people can upload to:

- Tops
- T-shirts
- Sweaters
- Dresses
- Skirts
- Pants
- Jeans
- Leggings
- Shorts
- Blazers
- Jackets
- Bags
- Shoes
- Accessories

Emma is truly in her element. She takes charge of everything just like a fashion director. Today, The Fashionist—tomorrow, *Vogue*.

Emma puts together three looks and Aisha photographs them so we will have content to populate the app. In the meantime, I work on a new function. I want to make the search feature better. It would be nice if you could create looks based on your mood or if you could pick your style, material, color, or occasion. I need to come up with an algorithm for this.

I explain to Emma that it is very important to get her input for the algorithm that decides on the combinations the app suggests to people when they upload their clothes. We need to tell the algorithm what are good combinations, and obviously I am not the one doing that. I just write her ideas into an algorithm.

Having Emma and Aisha here as part of the team is truly a game changer and is making the app even better than I thought it could be. I struggle through a few coding problems and can't help but think this is the exact thing I would have liked to brainstorm with Seven.

I look to see if he's online. His green dot is dark, black, and unavailable. In some ways, I guess he always was.

Can you go through a breakup with someone you've never even met and who was never even your boyfriend?

1:17 p.m.

Emma's mom reminds us that we need to eat lunch. Aisha wants Mexican. "Give me all the guac," she says. Emma is fine with that. I'm feeling—not hungry.

I decide that it's not healthy for Seven to cloud my mind like this. I'm going to send him one offline message just so we can end this like adults.

I send off a short message: "Can we talk?"

And then I wait.

In the meantime, Aisha brings up an awesome idea. She says that if we're going to do style inspiration in our app, users should be able to search through posts by body type. Genius.

But that's *another* algorithm. And since I'm the only coder on our team, getting all of this done is kind of stressing me out. Aisha is pretty good at math and offers to learn some basic coding so she can help me a little bit, but there's a lot she needs to learn before she can really contribute. Plus, her photography skills are crazy good, and we really need her focused on that.

8:36 p.m.

I have to go home, but first we come up with an official launch day for the app. Having a goal will help us keep our eye on the prize. We decide to launch in the first half of October—before winter break—so everyone can use it to get ready for all their holiday parties. That will give me enough time to make The Fashionist perfect and for Emma and Aisha to create enough "app-azine" content. We all set reminders on our phones: Launch app. We also agree to keep the app a secret between our giant little triangle of trust.

9:37 p.m.

No message from Seven—but honestly, I kind of forgot I even sent one.

12:30 p.m.

"We need a way for users to contact us if there's a problem," Emma says.

"And we should include a team photo—so it's more personal," Aisha says. "We can use the selfies we took in front of your door. They're cute." I'm just getting to know Aisha, but I know she loves a good selfie.

"They're not professional enough," Emma says.

I'll let them figure it out. I need to deal with the algorithms. I made a list this morning of everything we need to do, and we've got some serious work ahead of us if we want to meet our #appgoals.

2:50 p.m.

How long can a day last? How boring can a class be? If I want to know something about "The Gift of the Magi," I'll Google it.

I'm reminded that I'm still in high school. I may have a giant list of stuff to get done for The Fashionist, but I've also got three pages of history homework and an English literature essay due.

Wednesday, September 27

3:59 p.m.

Things that happened today: I got an A on my math test. So did River.

Things that did not happen today: My English literature paper. Soccer practice (because I skipped to get some work done on the app).

Friday, September 29

6:40 p.m.

My parents tell Finn and me over dinner that we're all going away October 13 for a long weekend.

"Work has been crazy, and I want to get away and spend some focused time together," my mom explains. I don't think my mom understands what crazy is.

We have to write down three places that we'd like to go and explain why. I really want to visit Europe—Paris or London or maybe Rome—but I know my parents will never go for it. I'm also worried about how my service will be there. If we plan to launch the app around that time, I'll need my phone.

I decide on:

1. Joshua Tree—because all of my favorite influencers take pictures there, and I think it's close to Coachella. I'll get enough content that my feed will be killer for at least a month.
2. San Francisco—because I want to go to the Mission District and check out cool bands and see musicians perform, plus it's close to Silicon Valley.
3. Miami Beach—because there's an art show going on at the same time and a lot of artsy people I follow are going there.

Monday, October 2

8:39 a.m.

I tell Emma and Aisha that we have a new deadline to get The Fashionist submitted to the App Store—in two weeks —before I leave on my trip. If we wait until after I get back, we'll lose too much time.

But it seems like the list of stuff I need to get done is growing. Emma mentions that we really need an official website to go along with the app. But we don't have much money. I may need to ask my parents.

3:01 p.m.

I don't have any more time to waste. I decide that if I'm going to figure out these algorithms, I need help. Since Seven has disappeared into the Internet, there's only one other person for me to ask: River.

As the dismissal bell rings, I see River walking ahead and speed up to catch her. "Hey River," I say, almost breathless. "Do you think you still have time to help us with our app?"

"Yeah, I should," she says.

"I'm getting tripped up on a few algorithms. Do you think we could talk tomorrow? Tonight I'm getting The Fashionist set up with a URL." I feel like I'm speaking her language, but my ego is quickly crushed.

"Yeah, sure. Just so you know, The Fashionist URL is already taken," River says with zero emotion.

"What do you mean?" I ask in a way that I'm nervously curious but optimistically hoping she's joking.

"I happened to look and saw that someone else had the URL," she says. "It doesn't look like they've updated in a while. It's like weird fashion links."

I start sweating from spots I didn't even know were possible to sweat from. I text Emma and Aisha and tell them we need to have an emergency meeting.

3:33 p.m.

I explain the problem as we're standing outside the cafeteria. Even though lunch has long been over, the hall still strangely smells like fried chicken sandwiches and pickles. We come up with a plan. We'll buy a different website for now, and River will set up an alert if the site renewal ever lapses. Then we can grab it. I just need to persuade my parents to front the money right away, so we can purchase that domain before it's gone. Since I'm asking for cash anyway, I'll also ask for money so that I can get a developer's account.

7:09 p.m.

My mom walks in the door and I bring up the money issue before she even sets her purse down, like maybe because her wallet is still close to her and she will just reach in and grab out the cash I need.

"For my app," I say.

"So this is why you've been spending so much time in your room," she says.

"Yeah," I answer, even though I know she isn't asking a question. She's coming to a realization.

Finn walks by and makes some dumb comment about why it isn't fair for my mom to give me money because she didn't give him any to buy new skates for hockey. Brothers are seriously overrated. I ignore him and explain to my mom that I need to get set up with a developer's account at Apple so I can get into the App Store. I also tell her that I need to register for a website, and kind of quickly, because apparently websites disappear.

My mom agrees to give me the cash and says that I will have to pay her back once the app starts making money. I don't know what surprises me more—that she fronts me the money or that she believes my app is going to be successful enough to make money one day. I text Emma and Aisha right away.

"Got the money."

I am so freaking excited. This is such a huge moment for us. I've always believed in the app, and it was great when Emma and Aisha did, too, but having my parents lend me the money shows me that they think my app idea is legit, too.

EMMA: Are you serious?

ME: Yah, totally.

AISHA: Our first round of funding? Wow, things just got real.

My stomach is doing somersaults I'm so happy. I wonder what other tech companies do when they secure an investor? Parents do count as investors, right? Yes, I decide, they sure do.

The surge in cash is giving me all the inspiration, but I can't do anything else on the app until I meet with River, so I try and distract myself. I make a list of things I need to do to prepare for vacation even though my parents still haven't told me where we're going.

Vacation list:
- Research spots to take photo inspirations for the app
- Research spots to take photos for my Instagram
- Look to see if they have a Longchamp store
- Figure out the best coffee shops
- Figure out where all of my favorite celebs went and then go there

Tuesday, October 3

6:04 p.m.

Our soccer team lost, which would normally annoy Emma—she's a total competitor—but today she doesn't seem to care. She wants to go back to her house and shoot some final outfits before we submit our app for approval.

She tells me about this idea that she and Aisha came up with to shoot a green velvet jumpsuit in front of an ivy-covered wall. "It's clutch," she says. River and I have been working on the algorithms today in-between classes (okay, full confession: in the middle of classes). Wait, I think we're actually on schedule to get this thing done.

8:13 p.m.
I really want to know where my parents are going to take us for the trip.

I check my mom's desk to see if I can find any printouts or information, but I don't come across anything except an electric bill and a receipt for hockey skates. I guess Finn got what he wanted after all.

Wednesday, October 4

6:32 p.m.
There are a pair of hiking boots on the table, and I'm confused.

My mom pulls some sort of casserole out of the oven, and my dad enthusiastically claps his hands. "I'm sure you guys would love to know what we've got planned," he says. "Well, let me give you a hint." He points to the hiking boots.

So maybe Joshua Tree, I think? But really, it could be anywhere. My parents enjoy doing things by foot, and I'm sure they would be those people wearing horrendous shoes even if we were going to San Francisco or Miami Beach.

But then my mom plops some odd yellow hiking equipment next to the boots, like this is some scavenger hunt to discover where we're going.

"Your mom and I are taking you to Rocky Mountain National Park," my dad says with the kind of smile that shows his teeth. When we don't say anything, he clarifies. "Colorado. We're going to Colorado!"

"We'll be kayaking and hiking and sleeping in a cabin together," my mom adds. Like that information is what will save this whole thing and somehow make it better. I want to know who wrote down Colorado.

"I'm sure you'll still be able to get some of those cute Instagrams you want," my dad says. My mom goes on to explain that she has a business trip right before our vacation that will take her to Denver. Because of that, she and my dad decided it would be best to combine the work trip and family trip into one.

Lovely.

I'm glad it's convenient for somebody.

Not.

Before I go up to my room, my dad gives me a pamphlet with all of the different things we'll be doing. There are pictures of mountains, snow, and rivers that look rough and intimidating and cold. There are special excursions to fly fish or study moose tracks. I don't see anything about a Longchamp store, an underground music scene, or spots where celebrities have taken amazing selfies. Also: There's a section about how to cook your own dinner over an outdoor fire.

That, plus the photo of families wearing matching orange polo shirts and khaki cargo pants on the front of the brochure makes me furious. I want to rip up the pamphlet and tell my parents that I'm not even going. 15 is definitely old enough to stay home alone for a few days.

8:11 p.m.

My phone buzzes. It's a text from Emma.

EMMA: My money's on Miami Beach.

I send her a photo of the pamphlet with the family in cargo pants, along with a string of angry emojis.

9:22 p.m.

You have a message from Seven.

The words pop up on my computer screen and might as well have been written in fireworks. I feel excited and overwhelmed and antsy.

SEVEN: Sorry that I've been MIA. I've been pretty busy with projects of my own, and I guess I was just upset you were working on the app without me. It kind of felt like our thing.

I always saw Seven as lucky (lucky number Seven!) but when he says "our thing," for some reason it rubs me the wrong way. Sure, Seven was an amazing support but the app has always been mine. I created it all on my own.

ME: Can we talk?

SEVEN: We are.

I can't tell if he's purposefully being funny to lighten the mood or just rude.

ME: Yeah, but I mean something off chat. Maybe Skype? I think talking online will only confuse things.

SEVEN: We should be able to figure something out. You should check out this site, codewithchris.com. I think it will really help you. How is your coding going, BTW?

ME: Really good, actually. After figuring it out myself, I'm about ready to launch.

Normally, I'm eager to impress Seven. But the lack of charm and easiness in our conversation changes that and leaves me feeling slightly rebellious. Instead of trying to come up with something cute to say, I want him to know I haven't been sitting around thinking about him and waiting for him to help me. Even if I sort of have.

SEVEN: Awesome. Did you add any new features? How did you work them out?

I tell him a little bit, and then he says he has to go but that he'll reach back out to set up a time to talk to me.

SEVEN: Good night, CharlieGirl. And really beautiful profile pic.

Maybe I'm supposed to feel flattered, but I'm just sort of over him. I don't have time for Seven and his ghosting. I have a business to run.

Thursday, October 5

7:10 p.m.

After soccer practice, I convince my mom to let me go over to Emma's for a little bit to "study." She may have infused our business with some cash, but she's still not totally into the idea of me spending chunks of a school night working on it. But River texted and was free to help me do a little bit of coding tonight, so I needed to make it happen. Together, we bang out the final pieces of the app. Now users can upload their entire closet, and it will create fun looks for them, either randomly or through an algorithm that lets you add in a keyword for the type of look you want. There's a search, there's a contact, there's a picture of us. Oh, and there's a form they can fill out if they have any issues. We can always add more features later, but this is a really great start.

I've been feeling tired and am about to head home when Aisha brings up something she found: There's going to be a Hackathon right in New York. She said it's a great way to meet other programmers and maybe even get the word out about our app. It's one day and it's free. But if you're under 18, you need a parent's permission.

How to convince my dad to let me go to something that has the word "hack" in the name? His email was just hacked two weeks ago, and he's still talking about it. This is going to be more complicated than asking my mom for money for our business.

8:11 p.m.

My dad's first response is no. He seemed to be in a good mood when he got home so I brought it up right away, but he said no way.

"But it will look great on a college application," I say. The education route usually works.

"She's only going to meet cute boys," Finn butts in. He hangs around just long enough to grab a bag of tortilla chips out of the cabinet.

"Let me think about," he says. "I'll talk to your mom."

I text Emma and Aisha. They both went the texting route. Their parents haven't responded yet.

10:01 p.m.

As one final check, I print out all the requirements to get our app in the App Store. There are a few things we're missing. I check the forum to ask around and see if all of these things are truly necessary.

Checking to see if Seven is there isn't my first thought. Progress. But there he is anyway. And he's suddenly changed his profile picture, too. It's like he wants me to see him since I changed mine. It's no longer a graphic. Instead, he kind of looks like—Justin Bieber? Really? A super-cute coder?

I screen snapshot Seven's photo on my phone and have zoomed in and looked at it a million times.

11:11 p.m.

I should be sleeping, but I can't help but wonder what Seven's real name could be: Brandon, Brad, Jude, Travis, John, Evan...

5:59 p.m.

Somehow, some way, my parents have decided that I can go to the Hackathon. Emma's and Aisha's parents are all on board, too. I've finally got something to look forward to. Something else to think about besides: Brandon, Brad, Jude, Travis, John, Evan...

(be) brave, not perfect

Reshma Saujani

#Fake

4

Saturday, October 7

2:45 p.m.

- Hackathon is tomorrow.
- App launch is 2 days away.
- Family vacation is 6 days away.

It's a busy week, and since I'm not thrilled to be packing woolly socks for Colorado, I'm wrapping up final edits for The Fashionist instead. I have a list on my wall of all the stuff that needs to be finished before I submit the app to the App Store for approval. I'm done with something, I cross it off with a giant purple marker. Best feeling ever!

Yesterday I got to cross off something huge: I officially created a developer's account. The only bummer part is that the account has to be in my mom's name. It's embarrassing but worth it, because now we can see our app in iTunes Connect. It's kind of like YouTube, but instead of uploading a video you upload your app. No one can see it but you, and it allows you to test out little things to make sure it's working correctly. Once everything is exactly like we want it to be, Apple gets a signal to review our app. Then if they approve it, we're in the App Store. We're so close!

My mom keeps coming into my room to talk to me about the trip. I give her 27 reasons why she should let me stay home alone. She gives me 27 reasons why I should be excited:

1. "It's important to do fun things as a family, Charlie!"
2. "Nature is good for you."
3. "You spend way too much time on your computer."
4. "Do you know how great being active is for your body?"

Blah. Blah. Blah. I'm just glad we're not going for a whole week.

The woods aren't really my scene, so I've already started faking a soccer injury. I told my parents that I fell during practice recently and have been hobbling around with a sore hip ever since. Every now and then, I sort of limp through the living room or kitchen. I'm hoping it will give me a good excuse to skip out on some of the hikes. I'd rather stay back in the cabin where I can keep tabs on all the rave reviews our app will be getting by then.

Sunday, October 8

8:23 a.m.

For a Sunday, I'm up early. But that's because it's Hackathon day. My dad agrees to let us all take a taxi so we won't have to muddle through the subway half asleep so early in the morning.

When we arrive, the room is buzzing with 150 young programmers. They've got tables with all kinds of breakfast foods for us, every kind of juice and flavored water imaginable, and trays stacked with snacks. Is this what it's like to work in tech? I'm so stoked.

Because I'm surrounded by a bunch of tech geniuses, I can't help but look around the room and wonder if Seven is any of these people. His photo was not super clear so he can still be anybody basically, like the guy looking awkwardly at the stage or another dude with wire-framed glasses and a short haircut.

Stop thinking about him, Charlie, I tell myself. You've got way more important things to deal with right now.

9:15 a.m.

The first Hackathon session is on the basics of programming. It feels good that I've gotten so fluent at coding that I'm long past the basics stage. But still, it's nice to have everything explained to us by experts who work for tech companies I'm obsessed with: Snapchat, YouTube, and Instagram. Next, we are assigned to teams, and I find out what project I'll be working on.

Okay, pinch me!

The person leading our group is a girl named Hailee who works at Snapchat—and I basically have a girl crush on her. Our project is to add a function to an app that will allow a local charity to be able to take donations right from the app. The team who finishes their code first wins.

After we get our assignment, but before we start coding, Hailee tells us a little bit about herself. She started coding when she was really young—her dad gave her a clunky black computer to play around on—and by the time she was 12, she had already made her first website. It was a fashion site where she broke down everything celebrities wore, where you could buy the clothes and accessories, and the photos always had a fun filter over them. It makes a lot of sense that she works for Snapchat, given the company kills it when it comes to fun filters.

She talks a lot about the struggles she's faced as a female coder, like how sometimes she's the only girl in the room. I'm so impressed by how open she is. She's so cool—and techie. Both things can be true.

We haven't been working for long when Hailee pulls me aside and asks me to join up with another group of more experienced programmers. I'm working on the same app but on a more complicated function. "It's River's table!"

I basically feel like someone gave me a million dollars. She recognized my coding skills. In a group full of people tapping away on their keys, she recognized my coding skills. Plus one, for me.

5:01 p.m.

We're still hacking it.

The guys from the coding club at school are here. River waves to one of them, a junior named Jack. She ignores the others. They ignore her, too. River tells me that apparently they're working on a music streaming app that only plays songs by bands that are local to our area. Everyone seems to be creating apps these days.

"We should all grab something to eat", Hailee says to River, me, and Emma who is at the next table. The day's about over and it's supposed to end with a dinner.

"Sure," Emma says. "That would be awesome."

Hailee answers all of our questions, and then she asks us some stuff. We tell her about The Fashionist. Talking to someone outside of our group about it feels thrilling, until she asks to see it. "You know, to take a quick peek at the code," she says.

I feel exposed. To outside eyes, the code probably looks unpolished and unclean. But it's not like I can say no, so I pull it up.

"This is pretty awesome stuff," she says. "You know, I love this floral-printed dress you girls posted on your inspiration board. If you created a function where you could earn money through affiliate links, you'd make money anytime someone buys something you post about." This is a game-changing piece of advice for The Fashionist!

Hailee says if we ever have any questions we can always email her. She also is happy to write up a review of the app to help spread the word. She has 100,000 followers—OMG!

Thoughts of Seven float into my mind. That isn't unusual—they often do. But this time what does feel unusual is how they feel. After experiencing how helpful Hailee is, I feel a little angry at him. He hasn't even reached out to set up our call. Seven always said he was helping me, but when I think about all the things he told me, they were often random and vague, and River ended up figuring them out. He asked questions, but otherwise, didn't have much to say. I thought he wanted me to think for myself, but if that was true, why did he get so angry at me when I did?

"Well, it was so nice to meet you," Hailee says. It jolts me back to reality and the crowded room in Chelsea.

6:35 p.m.

We all decide to celebrate the day by getting ice cream in cones shaped like sea creatures. We are in no rush to get home and decide to take the long way—across the Williamsburg Bridge. The city looks big, the air smells of exhaust, my friends are at my side, and I am thinking. High school is one moment and one place, but at times, it feels like your whole self has to fit inside of it. Meeting new people at the Hackathon—a boy with blue hair who created an online store where you can buy one-of-a-kind accessories for your sneakers and a girl who made a hilarious game that helps raise awareness around environmental conservation—made me realize there's a whole lot of world beyond my locker. I am excited for the future.

Maybe I should create an app that lets you count down the days until graduation?

8:13 p.m.

When I get home, my mom sends me to the store for bread. As I'm walking, it hits me that I might be self-sabotaging my situation with Seven. I had done it with Emma—saw things that weren't really there. Could I be doing that with him? I give it one more shot—a message in the dark, literally, I was on a dark corner of Sixth Street.

Me: I figured out how my app can make money. Finally.

This time, I didn't have to wait for a response.

SEVEN: Thumbs-up emoji. How?

Oh crap, my phone dies. Are you kidding me? Of all the times for my battery to give out! Figures. I rush into the store, grab the bread, and rush home to finish my conversation with Seven.

I hustle past the stores closing for the night and the fruit vendor selling chilled apples on the corner. I rush into my apartment, throw my bag and the bread on the counter, and bolt to my charger. While I wait for my phone to turn on, I flip open my computer. I log on so quickly my fingers barely touch the keys. Too late, Seven is offline. Everything feels dark again.

Monday, October 9

8:00 a.m.

I have never been more happy that today is Columbus Day. This is such a perfect long weekend. First the Hackathon and then another day off being able to work on the app. Yeah.

9:20 p.m.

Well, I didn't hit the Monday goal, but I'm close to releasing the app. I need to:
1. Have 10 people try out the beta version to make sure it works perfectly.
    Two more to go!
2. Make sure The Fashionist brand name is available.
    Aisha is checking.
3. Officially register our app as a company.
    Emma and I are doing it tomorrow.

11:01 p.m.

Sometimes, even when I'm exhausted, sleeping is still hard because I keep thinking about all of the little problems we have with the app. How long should I spend developing an app? Maybe I should hold off for a year and make it even better. There aren't a lot of teen app developers for a reason.

My phone beeps.

SEVEN: Tell me about how you're going to make money off of this app, genius?

Every time I get annoyed enough with Seven that I think I'm kind of over him, there he is again. I send a few lines that Hailee had told me, and say I will talk to him tomorrow. I need to get some sleep.

: SEVEN: OK. Good night. BTW, did I tell you that I love your new profile pic? So
pretty. –T

And now I'm actually supposed to be able to fall asleep?

Tuesday, October 10

8:12 a.m.

Awake, kind of. I realize that Seven signed his message last night with a "T." I
start to imagine what his real name could be. Thomas.... Tristan.... Taylor....
Tom.... Tyler...

10:11 a.m.

Emma, Aisha, and I are supposed to be researching whom we're going to write
our women's history paper about, but instead our focus is on the app.

"I can't believe that it's almost time for people to learn about it," Emma says.
"It's crazy that people we know could just start downloading it and using it."

Up until this point, we had managed to keep it a secret.

"Are you nervous, Charlie?" Emma asks and looks around to make sure no
one is in earshot.

"No, not really," I say, trying to sound chill. "You haven't told anyone about
our plans have you?"

"Not a soul," Aisha says.

Emma shakes her head no.

Just then Aisha gets a message from a guy named Alex whom she met at the
Hackathon. He was one of the guys who created the web sneaker shop. Her face
is so red, I can feel it.

"Do you like him?" It feels weird to be talking about anything but the app
right now, but I ask Aisha anyway. To be a good friend.

"He's just so smart and funny," Aisha says. "Plus, you saw how cute he is,
right? He's basically everything."

The conversation veers toward Aisha and Emma talking about whether they
think Aisha and Alex are going to hook up. It brings back all the uncomfortable
feelings I have about high school. I may have created an app earlier than most,
but when it comes to kissing, dating, and making out, these conversations

76

make it clear that I'm later than most.

Feeling left out, I decide to tell them about Seven.

"So I've been talking to a guy, too," I say.

It's Aisha who responds first. "Really, who?"

"He's a coder I met," I say, keeping it intentionally vague that I met him online. For all they know, I met him at the Hackathon. "His name is Seven." I realize after I say it that his name is not, in fact, Seven.

"Oh, really?" Aisha says in a playful voice. "Where did you meet him?"

I don't want to lie. So I don't.

"I actually met him in this online coding forum," I say super quickly so I don't change my mind.

Emma wastes no time. "Online? Seriously, Charlie?" That's kind of creepy. He could be like a catfish or something. Have you met him in person? Do you know where he lives or even how old he is? Or if he's some weirdo man on a boat in the middle of the sea sending you messages?"

There isn't a way I can come up with a lie fast enough to make this all sound good, so I don't.

"Well, I know that his first name actually isn't really Seven," I say. "And the other stuff, well, no, I don't know everything exactly. At least, not yet. We're usually so busy talking about code that we don't have a ton of time to talk about little details."

I know how bizarre it sounds as the words leave my mouth.

"Little details?" Emma sounds like she's in disbelief. "Those aren't just little details, Charlie. That's normal stuff to know about someone. If he doesn't want you to know, it's because he's hiding something."

"It really is kind of weird," Aisha says. "I feel like he's some sicko who's probably 50-years-old and likes to talk to young girls on the computer. It's not safe."

"Tell me why he doesn't tell you anything personal," Emma demands.

"Because he's too busy trying to help me with the app." And as I say it, I can only hope that it's true.

I need to save the conversation—and fast.

"Let's make a pact," I say. "The next time I talk to Seven, I will make sure he gives me all of this information, like his personal social media accounts and stuff, or I won't talk to him anymore but you both need to cut him a break. Do you remember the idea about making money off our app?"

Aisha and Emma both nod their heads yes in unison.

"Well, that was his idea," I say, so proudly that you would think I believe it.

"Seriously? I thought Hailee came up with that idea." I didn't think it would be Aisha who calls my bluff.

"No, it was Seven and I just ran the idea by her," I say. "If Seven was some bad guy, why would he want to help us like that?"

It seems to calm them both down.

And then because I just couldn't let it go, I added that Seven had a friend at the App Store who was going to make sure our approval went through in record time. "It's the best app he's seen in a long time," I said.

I should have stopped talking.

1:45 p.m.

I'm in math class with River, and luckily, we have a project that requires us to be on the computer. While everyone else is stressing over midterms, there we are—secretly planning the launch of a company, which makes me forget about my earlier conversation with Emma and Aisha. Being with River is so easy, sometimes our conversations involve nothing but code.

We crossed everything off the list and are in the final testing stages of app development. We put each function to its total limits to make sure it does what we need it to. A few problems pop up, but we fix them quickly. River jokes that my eyebrows always go up in a serious arch when I'm coding.

"Tomorrow's the day," River says. "It's ready. Let's set the app to review and see if Apple approves it."

It's a decision that feels big enough to tip the world. You would think confetti is about to fall from the clouds, but nothing happens. We agree that it's time, and I pack up to go to English class.

2:39 p.m.

I start second-guessing whether the app is really ready. I tell my worries to Emma and Aisha.

"Listen, we can stall forever, but we just need to do it," Aisha says.

"I remember Hailee saying that there will always be a list of changes," Emma adds.

"The foundation is solid—even River thinks so," Aisha says.

And they're right. The more I look at the app, the more things I notice that can change. Once our app is live, we can see what users think of it and what changes they would like to see.

"Sometimes you have to give yourself a pep talk. Like hello you're a queen, don't be sad, and you're doing great…"

It's time to do this.

My metamorphosis.

Wednesday, October 11

7:15 a.m.

Today's the day!

9:30 a.m.

We all decide not to submit the app review first thing and set it to happen at 3 p.m. EST. That's noon in California, which feels like the ideal time—not first thing in the morning when everyone is busy and not at the end of the day when it can get overlooked or ignored.

3:00 p.m

I thought every moment of the day would feel monumental—the last time I'd eat lunch in the cafeteria before launching my app, the last time I take an algebra test before being the CEO of a tech company, the last time I walk down the hallways as just Charlie. All day I feel ready! I am ready to see our hard work acknowledged.

Aisha, Emma, River, and I finally gather around my laptop.

River says I should do the honors.

"One, two...," we all say together.

My finger hovers above the button. Never did it feel like the click of a mouse could change so much.

"Three," we all say. We stare at the screen for I don't even know how long. I don't even know if we remember to breathe.

Aisha pops us out of our trance. "Let's all go to Juice Gen and get some smoothies to celebrate." It's such an Aisha thing to say—she's obsessed with any drink that's green, but it actually sounds good.

Now we have to wait to find out if we will be approved. Everything feels perfect. In fact, it feels *so* good, it feels impossible to feel bad. Little do I know, I'm about to be that girl again – the one with the electric-red drink spilled down the front of her bathing suit. Metaphorically, but still.

6:01 p.m.

We're so amped up that we all decide to head back to my apartment and hang out for a few hours before we each have to retreat to our bedrooms to finish up the papers we have due tomorrow.

We're all talking at the same time and saying the same thing. "When would we get a response from Apple? Would our app be in the App Store tomorrow? Wednesday? Thursday? Never?"

I'm leaving on my trip soon, and even though I should have Internet, Emma promises me she'll check her email every five minutes and send me a text as soon as there's any news. Emma's family is staying in town for the short holiday. Aisha's parents are one step away from being hippies and taking her on a phone-free retreat in upstate New York, so she will have to wait.

6:23 a.m.

I wake up with one sock half off and my vision a bit blurry. The sound of the garbage truck rattling down the block is right outside my window. I remember about the app and I grab my phone off my nightstand and scroll to the App Store. So far, there are no results for The Fashionist.

No mail from Apple.

No changed status in iTunes Connect.

And it stays that way for the rest of the day.

8:14 a.m.

I quickly scan my emails one last time before we board our flight to Colorado, and I have to put my phone in airplane mode.

Nothing.

Why do parents choose such early flights?

Why did school allow me to be off anyway? They are always super strict but suddenly when my parents ask if I can be off for something I don't even want, it is ok? Really?

11:34 a.m.

Location check-in is a mountain somewhere in Colorado.

I had looked up online photos of Colorado before we left and I saw pictures of the Kardashians and Gigi Hadid skiing, so I was feeling hopeful. But when we pull up to our winter bungalow and are met by a man named the Colorado Captain, I start to lose hope.

The winter bungalow is more like a wooden hut.

The Colorado Captain tells us about all the wonderful "features" of the bungalow—he's careful not to use the word *amenities*. There's a firepit in the front to cook your food and a new bucket water system, so you'll have hot water to take a shower. "But you'll need to wait at least seven minutes for it to heat up," the Colorado Captain says, chuckling.

There isn't a whiff of Wi-Fi anywhere. I completely freak out. How am I supposed to check my email so I can find out if we won? We don't even have service, so I won't be able to get a text message from Emma. It's not like I'm anywhere international or cool that would make this all worth it. I'm in the middle of freaking Colorado. I storm through the hut, complaining and trying to convince my parents to move us to a hotel.

My parents totally ignore my outburst.

"Well, look at that—there is a little burner to make coffee," my dad says.

"Wonderful! I did bring our French press and coffee beans," my mom said. "Did you and Finn see the fireplace?"

"I'd love to get out there and do some exploring—the smell of those pine trees is calling me—but I'm sure we're all a bit tired. I can boil us some water for hot cocoa first if you want," my dad adds.

I don't want hot chocolate. I want Wi-Fi.

Finn, who is the lamest of lame, just got back from taking a quick walk around our wilderness of an area and he tells me to follow him.

"I'm not in the mood, Finn," I say.

"Stop being so dramatic, Charlie, and just follow me," he says. He walks toward a building with a green roof that the Colorado Captain had called the front desk. As we walk closer, I see that there is a desk in the front of the room with a woman sitting at it whose job looks like nothing more than to tell you hello when you check in and goodbye when you check out.

"They have Internet," Finn says.

I don't believe him. It would be so like Finn to pull a terrible joke on me, but he walks us inside and I see that he's telling the truth. There isn't Wi-Fi and I still won't be able to get cell service or receive any text messages, but they have an ivory cube of a computer in the far corner and the woman says I can use it once a day.

"We discourage the use of technology here in the hopes that people will choose to connect with nature instead of their devices so we limit it, but we understand some people have business to attend to," she explains. "You seem a little young for that, but no discrimination here. You can check once a day just like everyone else." Apparently she does say more than hello and goodbye.

"Why don't you get out there and try the ropes course? You should smell the fresh air and check your mail later." She gives me the kind of smile that's nice but is also telling me to leave.

I step outside and she's right. I take a deep breath and feel myself balloon a bit with a crispness that pinkens my skin and reddens my nose. I feel so much better. I'm not sure if it's the air—or the comfort of knowing there's a computer close by.

1:30 p.m.
We go into the nearby town to get lunch, and afterward my dad does get us on the ropes course. It starts in a thicket of bushy pine trees that seem to sweep my skin when I walk by, as if they're trying to remove whatever stress, anxiety, and insecurity I had before walking in there. Once I start zipping through the trees, I eventually get to a part that opens up. I see faraway mountains all glowing so white with snow they look lunar. As I land on the final platform near a wet zone, the smell in the air is changed to wet earth.

I wait for my dad to come flying in and I notice a patch of sunlight sneaking through the pine needles, making the forest look like it's covered in diamonds. For about three seconds, I think it looks cool—almost like a very woodsy Snapchat filter—but as soon as my mind goes to Snapchat, I start to think about whether The Fashionist is in the store.

I have my phone in my back pocket and check for a signal but nothing.

We're done, so we walk back to the hut and my mom tells us about the campfire meal she's cooking for us tonight. My first order of business is to hit the front desk. But as I get closer, I notice the windows are dark. Crap. The sign on the door says closed at 5 p.m. and open at 7 a.m. If I squint hard enough, I can see the chunk of a computer cast off alone in the corner. So close, yet so far.

I can't believe there are places in America that still don't have Wi-Fi. What kind of first-world country are we?

7:15 p.m.

My Brooklynite mom's idea of a campfire meal is cheese fondue. As it bubbles, and the fire crackles, and the light dances, it feels like we're cocooned in the last bit of warmth and light in the world. It's cozy and relaxing, and I actually don't mind it.

No sounds of messages to make my nerves jump. No group texts stressing me out about all the things we have to do for the app. No Snapchat streaks to keep up with. Nothing, and it feels okay for at least one night.

Saturday, October 14

7:04 a.m.

There's a thin layer of frost on the grass that makes the green blades crunch as I dash over to the building. The walk over leaves a path of footprints that looks like I left a permanent trail in the grass. It's very early, when the moon is there—but almost not—and the sky is turning blue.

I am in! I log in quickly, still a little skeptical that the Internet will actually work, but it does, and no mail from Apple. Our status in iTunes Connect hasn't changed, either. I type a quick message to Emma and Aisha, letting them know my phone doesn't have service and my Internet time is limited. Hopefully Aisha is able to go online via a laptop on her phone-free retreat so she can still read my message.

Maybe Apple thinks our app is too lame to get back to us or maybe it's just the weekend and this kind of stuff doesn't get approved on the weekend. It's got to be that. I know our app is not lame.

8:51 a.m.

I have to fuel up because we're going on a hike. In my excited and sarcastic voice because they're both the same, I ask my family, "Who knew you could make banana pancakes on a fire?"

5:21 p.m.

We're back at the hut, but it's too late for Wi-Fi at the front desk and using it again today would break the rules anyway. About halfway through the hike, I tried my fake-hip-injury trick in hopes I'd be allowed to head back a little earlier. But because we were doing a loop, the guide just left me sitting on a rock alone without any phone reception because I had checked about 51 times.

7:03 a.m.

Off I go, across the crunchy grass to huddle over the computer again. The keyboard is missing a "T" and "L" and the "C," "S," and "A." We have one more day here, and I'm not sure how much longer this computer is going to last.

OMG! What? Why? Our app was turned down. I am in disbelief and shocked! I want to cry, but my tears stay lodged behind my eyes like cement droplets, heavy and unwilling to move.

But I don't have time to figure out what happened or even to message Emma or Aisha. We're due on our kayaking trip, and I can't let my parents know that I've been sneaking on the Internet.

9:12 a.m.

We have to hand in our cell phones at the start of the kayaking course, and I don't even care. I also wouldn't care if the bubbly, wild water took my phone and washed it completely away—and my lousy app that's on it.

4:44 p.m.

It's late afternoon, and we just got back from our kayaking adventure—if that's what you want to call it.

I'm cold and shivering because, at one point, our boat tipped over. We were almost back to shore when Finn began paddling like a wild person, and our boat started wobbling and then dumped us into the choppy water. My dad tried to keep our spirits high by saying things like, "Let's do this, warriors." Meanwhile, my mom was pointing out the gorgeous trees, gorgeous mountains, gorgeous sky, and gorgeous streams along the way. Everything was gorgeous.

From my view, the world sucked.

8:45 p.m.

The reality about The Fashionist being denied had been weighing on me. Every now and then, it would touch me and I would feel it, but for the most part, it still felt far away and unreal. But lying in my flannel sleeping bag, no light, no sound, no smell of pine trees—my failure is the only thing that's here. The tears heave out like vomit. I'm looking forward to getting to Denver tomorrow. We agreed that we would spend one day exploring the more bustling side of Colorado before we have to go home.

My dad pokes his head into my little room. "Are you sleeping, Charlie?"

"No."

I wonder if he heard my sniffles. The walls are as thin as paper.

"Can you pop out here for a second?"

I climb out of my sleeping bag and shuffle my feet into the main room. There's a furry carpet. I never stare too closely at it because I don't want to realize that at one point it was an actual animal.

"We've decided to have a vote about whether we should leave early and go to Denver tomorrow or spend one more day in the national park," he says. "Your mom and I feel like we've all been having such a good time, and it's been so nice to not be tethered to our phones, that we thought it might be better to meander around here."

It seems like everyone already discussed it without me, because they immediately vote and all three of them, Finn included, raise their hands to stay.

I don't even put my hand up to vote no. I just back into my little room. Just another typical example of the fake democracy in our family. My father only suggests voting if he knows the outcome will be in his own interest.

8:52 p.m.

Finn knows how upset I am because he asks me to do something he never does: He invites me to a party. First the Internet and now this. What is in this pine tree air?

"I met some people when we were kayaking today and they're staying in the little town," he says. "Do you want to come? It will be better than sitting around here with nothing to do."

I'm not sure why Finn is inviting me. Maybe it's because he knows if I go, my mom and dad will give him the green light to be out. The idea starts to make me mad when he interrupts my emotion.

"Listen, I think the place will have Wi-Fi," he says. "It's at a hotel a few miles away."

That's all I need to hear.

Our parents agree to let us stay out until 11 p.m.

9:16 p.m.

The party is everything I hate. The hotel room appears smoky, even though I don't see anyone smoking. There's music playing so loud it forces you to stand closer to people than you would ever want. There's a table in the center of everything covered with cheap, half-full beer bottles, probably because the people guzzling them got too sick to even finish. It's not my scene. I pull out my laptop and set up as far away from everyone as I can. The one time I'm happy to be invisible.

Yes, I'm able to get online. It makes being forced to watch Finn shamelessly flirt with a girl almost worth it. I log into my email and see messages from Emma. She knows that our app got denied and sent a message with a million sad emojis.

I'm about to go and find Finn when I realize that my phone is ringing. It's Emma trying to FaceTime.

"Oh my God! Emma!" I say it louder than I probably need to, but the music only seems to be getting louder.

"Charlie, I am so glad I got ahold of you," Emma says. "I've been dying over here, dealing with all of this alone. I did get an email back from Aisha, so she knows, but I haven't heard anything else."

"I let everyone down," I say.

"You really didn't, Charlie. But wait, where are you?"

"I'm at a party with Finn. I know, it's weird, and it's not what you think. I basically came for the Wi-Fi."

"How are you feeling?"

"This is all killing me. I want to be back in New York. But listen, I'm going to figure out why the app was denied. Maybe there's something we can do?"

I realize I may have some explaining to do about why Seven's "friend" wasn't able to secure us an approval, but I decide to deal with that later.

"Wait, so you don't know?"

"No," I say. "Do you?"

"Yes, that's what the strangest part is. We were denied because..."

And just like that, Emma's face disappears from the phone. Ugh. The Wi-Fi must have gone out, and I can't get my phone to reconnect. I want to fling all the empty beer cans right off the counter. What was the weird part? Why were we denied?

I have to find Finn.

10:03 p.m.

It hasn't been that long, but it's already too late and for some terrible reason Finn decided to drink. His body is loose but he also feels like dead weight.

"My head is spinning, Charlie," Finn says. When he says spinning, it takes him awhile to stop making the "ing" sound.

My head is spinning, too. But not because I've been drinking—but because I can't get over what Emma said. Why wasn't our app approved?

Think, Charlie. You need to deal with this emergency first.

I persuade the front desk at the hotel to call us a taxi. I'm still furious that Finn has been drinking. "Mom and Dad are going to kill you, Finn," I say. I want him to feel some of the stress I'm feeling, but he's already asleep with his head against the window.

Somehow, I get him back inside the hut without waking our parents and shove him onto his bed without even taking off his shoes. I grab my sleeping bag from my room and sleep on the floor to make sure he's okay.

Monday, October 16

7:46 a.m.

It's the trickle of light coming into the room that first gets me to open my eyes, but it's the sound of my parents' voices that keeps me from closing them. They're talking to Finn and it doesn't sound good. With everyone awake, I wonder how I'm going to get to the front desk to check my email.

When I walk into the main room to get a feel for the situation, my dad says we're immediately leaving the hut. We'll make a quick stop in Denver, but then we'll be heading home. In a way, Finn came through for me again.

10:25 a.m.

I know we're back in the real world when my phone shows full service. I go right to the email from Apple.

It lists a few reasons that I understand: I used "test" four times in the app and that's not allowed. *Ugh, what a dumb mistake.* When Apple was testing the app, it received a number of error messages in the shopping cart feature. *Okay, that can be easily fixed.* We didn't ask our users for permission to use their location. *I can fix that, too.* The app crashed in a previous version of iOS. *That problem freaks me out a little, but I'm sure I can figure it out.*

But it was the last reason that completely threw me.

"Your app was denied because it already exists in the App Store."

I can feel tiny waves of relief rolling in my stomach. It's all just a mistake, some sort of misunderstanding. I had checked. Our app is the first of its kind.

I keep reading.

"Additionally, it appears that The Fashionist is constructed from the exact same code as Dressed, the app we're referencing, so you're in violation of the App Store's intellectual property rules."

Now I know there's a mistake.

I go to the App Store and look it up right away. It can't be right. I did research on all the similar apps out there and am confident our idea is one-of-a-kind. But there it is—Dressed. I see the name of the app developer: Theo Seven.

I don't want
fear of
failure
to stop me
doing what
I really
care about

Emma Watson

#Fighter

11:34 a.m.
There are some moments in life, that when they happen, you will never forget where you were.

Where were you when you found out Prince Harry and Meghan Markle got engaged?
Sitting in my math class.

Where were you when the last president was elected?
Hanging out at Emma's house.

Where were you when you heard Taylor Swift's new album had dropped?
In bed, barely awake.

Where were you when you realized that the person you kind-of-sort-of-maybe liked had been lying to you for months and was only interested in your code—not you?
About to board an airplane in Denver, Colorado.

How am I going to explain this to Emma and Aisha?

The worst part is that I don't even know exactly what I'm sad about or what hurts the most. That my dreams of getting my app into the App Store have been ruined or that I'm experiencing my first relationship letdown with someone that I don't even know. I guess I'm sad about all of it.

1:34 p.m.
Realizing what Seven had done starts as a slow burn, but turns into a hot rage as I look out the window from 30,000 feet. Everything looks so tiny, except my problem which still seems huge.

6:10 p.m.
Landed. I text Emma and Aisha.
- ME: Let's talk tomorrow. I've got updates.

What I have to say can only be done in person.

8:35 a.m.

Homeroom feels like a confessional and this is my moment of truth. Hopefully, forgiveness follows.

I explain everything about Seven—how often I've been communicating with him, exactly what I know about him, and also how I completely lied about him having a friend at Apple. I share that I thought of Seven as a friend and an ally, someone who truly wanted to help me be a better coder and create the best app possible. I explain that my judgment was probably clouded, as it began to feel like we were moving from friends into something more. At some point along the way, I didn't really need Seven to help me code anymore. In fact, I never really needed him—I taught myself and developed amazing skills of my own. I didn't have a boyfriend to kiss between classes. I had something better—someone who liked what I liked.

I also tell them I was wrong.

I wait. And get ready for them to dump me, too.

But then I was wrong. Again.

"I am honestly so sorry, Charlie," Emma says. "He is terrible and completely played you. I know you were probably expecting me to say, 'I told you so,' but honestly, I see how you got sucked in. This is his fault, not yours."

"Yeah, we were worried about your safety, but no one could have ever predicted that he would do something like this," Aisha says.

"We're not going to let him go down without a fight," Emma says. "Why don't we try to contact Hailee from the Hackathon? Surely she has some advice for us, and she said we could reach out anytime."

"And you know what, we developed one app, so if we have to we'll develop another one," Aisha adds.

"But I really do think that Hailee can help us," Emma says.

This is what friendship looks like—steady, solid, supportive, and fierce.

And as for Seven—forget him. He doesn't deserve me.

9:34 a.m.

The first chance I get, I write the email.

. . . .

Hi Hailee,

I don't know if you remember me, but we met at the Hackathon. I was working on the app that would allow charities to accept donations electronically. Before the Hackathon I had also developed my own personal app, The Fashionist, and I showed it to you. Well, we submitted it to the App Store, and it turns out that someone I trusted had been copying my code all along and submitted it before I did. We were denied. Obviously, my friends and I are extremely upset that all the hard work we did was for nothing. But we don't want to give up. Can you give us any advice?

Thanks.
Charlie

. . . .

I'm back to waiting again.

Wednesday, October 18

6:15 p.m.

I went to soccer practice. I aced my English lit test. I ate a taco salad for lunch. I stared at the wall and waited for the bell to ring in government class. Everything is back to normal.

But it's also not normal at all.

I can't stop checking my email to see if Hailee has responded. (Spoiler alert: She hasn't.) And I also can't stop looking at the App Store to see if Dressed is getting good ratings. So far, not much traction. I can't decide if that's a good or bad thing. Does that mean our idea was terrible?

6:58 a.m.

I wake up to a message from Hailee!

• •

My bad for emailing you back so late! I was on a trip and trying not to check my email. Anyway, WTH? I can definitely help you out. Let's set up a time to FaceTime, and you can tell me more.

• •

6:58 p.m.

It's been 12 hours since I got Hailee's message, and boy have things changed. After explaining everything to Hailee on a call, she looked into it and found out that Seven has been in trouble before for cloning successful apps—Hailee said that's tech speak for copying. In fact, his apps have been removed from the store seven times before. How fitting.

The good news is that Hailee has friends on the Apple team and is working with them to have Dressed taken down, as long as we can provide the paperwork of when we filed for our company name and all of the coding correspondence we had with Seven. I sent everything over to her earlier, and now I'm just waiting again.

The Fashionist still has a chance.

Friday, October 20

5:10 p.m.

There were so many reasons why it shouldn't have happened today.

- It was the end of the day, right before the weekend.
- It had been less than 48 hours since we filed our complaint with Apple.
- I wasn't sure the chat screenshots I had with Seven were enough to prove the idea was ours.

But it happened, and the feeling was even better than I could have imagined.

The Fashionist is now available for download in the App Store, and Dressed is nowhere to be seen.

Emma, Aisha, and I screamed, jumped, danced, and turned various shades of pink and red.

The thought of losing my business had been almost too much to bear. I had worked too hard and come too far. It's scary that someone can just come along and try to copy something that belongs to you. Let alone the fact that I almost lost my BFF! But today—we prevailed. Yes!

To celebrate, we decide to go to one of our favorite restaurants, the Sugar Factory American Brasserie in the Meatpacking District in Manhattan. We toast with giant Lollipop Passion drinks served in cups as big as bowls, and order baskets of fries, macaroni and cheese pops, and a giant sundae topped with sparklers.

In-between bites, we keep opening up our phones to look at the app. We've been looking at it for weeks, but in the App Store it still looks different. It looks—real. I guess it didn't before. There's even a little button next to it that says Get It Now.

Anyone can download it this very minute. Someone in Chicago or Los Angeles, or even Australia, could be looking at the app and trying it. We decide to go through the alphabet and list all the different places that someone might be using it.

"Let's start with A," I say with a mouth full of sweet juices and white chocolate sauce.

"Anywhere," Emma shouts.

That seems so right and complete, we didn't go any further than that.

Anybody, anywhere could be using our app.

11:10 p.m.

There have already been 16 downloads for the app!

Okay, so 9 of them were from Emma, Aisha, and me, and our parents. But that still means there were 7 genuine downloads.

7?

Ugh. I hate that number.

I text Finn and tell him to get the app even though he will never use it.

11:59 p.m.

I check the downloads one more time before going to sleep. There's a new one from Jack—one of the guys in the coding club who I'm pretty sure has a thing for Emma. I know it's him because he left a message on our social media account saying "he's excited to see it." That makes 8 random downloads. It feels so incredible, it might as well be the whole world.

Saturday, October 21

1:11 a.m.

I have insomnia but really it's just excitement. I'm obsessed with checking to see if we have anymore downloads (we don't) or if there are any reviews (there aren't).

I do see that Jack started following not only The Fashionist social media account but also my personal ones. I wonder why he's so interested in connecting with me now. I start to get paranoid that he's a spy for the coding club. They're working on some kind of app, too.

I click on his social media accounts.

I see pictures of him at concerts. There's another post he's tagged in after a 5K through Central Park—he has on black shorts and is biting a gold medal. He follows a bunch of musicians and also a bike company that he's apparently obsessed with (he likes all of their posts), and he went on a trip to London last year with his family. His recent status updates show he thinks cronuts are overrated, is bummed that his favorite jean shop on Mott Street has shut down, spent last Saturday in Connecticut helping his grandfather restore a sailboat, and desperately needed some help on his math homework exactly two weeks and three days ago.

Sunday, October 22

6:49 p.m.

My parents are super proud of The Fashionist team and took us all out to dinner. They toast to us and wear smiles as bright as lightbulbs. Sometimes everything feels so surreal that you need the enthusiasm in other people to truly feel it.

I felt it.

"You're a real go-getter," my dad says. My mom gives us all a huge hug. Finn was back to being Finn—but he did download the app.

9:01 p.m.
Time now feels measured in downloads, and at the moment, things seem stalled. We have no new users. After a group text with Emma and Aisha, we decide that we need to get everyone at school on board. They send out messages to everyone they know.

10:13 p.m.
One new download. It's River. She also sends me a DM:

• •

"Awesome."

• •

For River, that actually says a lot.

Monday, October 23

8:35 a.m.
Dang, Emma and Aisha are on it and have started really generating publicity for the app. Not only is the majority of our school talking about it, but they're also telling us how awesome it is—we now have 32 new downloads.

It's so cool—I did this. It's like people are carrying around a little piece of my idea in their pocket and it's helping them feel good about themselves every day—such a fire feeling.

2:22 p.m.
Out of the blue, Jack slides into my DMs.

It's a picture of his feet—he's wearing old-school Adidas—and there's a text box that asks if I want to hang out this weekend and study for the big science test. I feel a pit in my stomach that I've experienced before. This time I recognize the worry and apprehension as something I should pay attention to.

I'm sure that Jack's only messaging me because he wants to get closer to Emma. Maybe he thinks I'll bring her, and even if I don't, he can ask me a bunch of questions and learn more about her.

"Busy," I respond to Jack.

And I am busy—being a total tech boss and building an app.

39 total downloads.

Tuesday, October 24

8:37 p.m.

Taking control with Jack has caused a shift in me. It's very slight, but I feel like I've taken some of my power back, something that it seemed like Seven had stolen. There's just one thing I need to get a better handle on: stopping the random thoughts of Seven that pop up. I think about him less. I don't get jumpy anymore when I see I have a new message on my phone. But I still feel like I don't have closure.

I log on to my messaging app and type:

"Can we please talk?"

I delete, delete, delete until the message is gone.

"Are you T. Swift?"

Delete, delete, delete.

"Why are you such a horrible person?"

Delete, delete, delete.

I wish it were that easy to delete him from my mind.

Wednesday, October 25

11:40 a.m.

We're up to 68 downloads, but we need more.

Some of our ideas to raise more awareness: hang up posters at our school, create a contest where you could win a styling session with Emma if you get a friend from another school to sign up, talk to our principal to see if he'll post about it on the school's main web page, and approach the student newspaper about doing a story on us.

2:13 p.m.

Our entire school is plastered in The Fashionist posters, and they seem to be working. We're up to 218 downloads. People are definitely into our app, and they're also really into something else: coding.

So many girls are coming up to me and want to know how I made The Fashionist, how I learned to code, and how someone would even begin. One girl told me that I've really inspired her.

~~Invisible.~~

Inspiring.

10:34 p.m.

311 total downloads.

One new text from Jack.

JACK: Are you still interested in joining coding club? We may have a spot opening up?

ME: No, I'm actually pretty busy.

Saturday, October 28

7:30 a.m.

I'm up early to meet Emma for our soccer game. We're in the running for playoffs. I secretly hope we don't make it.

10:55 a.m.

Game over.

And maybe our season, too.

We lost, but whether we make it into the playoffs depends on how the other teams do.

I sit in the steamy locker room, hair wet and stuck to my face, and think about how I'm so glad the soccer season is over—at least, it probably is over. I tried it and it's just not for me. I want to spend my time doing more STEM things, like starting up a coding club for girls at school. I make a note in my phone to send an email to our principal about what I have to do to get that started.

11:41 a.m.

We stop at H&M on the walk home to see some of their newest stuff. Emma wants to get some inspiration for new posts for The Fashionist.

12:37 p.m.

To help us meet our #appgoals, we need a stage bigger than our school. So we're at Aisha's, putting together a list of well-known websites and magazines we can contact to let them know about our app.

So far we have:

- *Seventeen*
- Refinery29
- Man Repeller
- *Lenny Letter*
- *Rookie*
- *Teen Vogue*

We draft up a sample email to send out.

. . . .

Dear Man Repeller,

We are three teens—Charlie, Emma, and Aisha—and we've developed an app that helps you get dressed fabulously every day. No matter what's in your closet, or how much time you have, you will leave your house every day looking like the ultimate cool girl.

We're new and don't have a ton of downloads yet, but would absolutely love your support. Would you consider reviewing our app and sharing it with your readers? We are positive that they will love it.

X

The Fashionists

. . . .

3:33 p.m.

I put a callout on Instagram asking users to tag #thefashionistftw in a post for a chance to win a styling session with Emma.

3:49 p.m.

I check to see if anyone is using the hashtag. Not really. But we still have 11 new followers on The Fashionist account and 3 new downloads of the app.

4:16 p.m.

We decide we need to start paying attention to the analytics, so we know what users enjoy reading about the most. So far, jeans and vintage sneakers have the most clicks.

To state the obvious: We decide to create new posts around jeans and vintage sneakers.

My favorite thing to do is to tweak the app and make it better, but I get a thrill out of all the other stuff that we have to do to keep the business running, too. There are a lot of moving pieces to keep a business running smoothly and it's all fun in different ways. Plus, I get to do all of this with my friends.

4:44 p.m.

Aisha has a new idea: She says we should create inspiration boards based on the weather. So if it's nice outside, mostly playful dresses should pop up. If it's going to snow, puffer jackets and chic snow boots should appear. Users should be able to do that in search, too.

I quickly put together an algorithm to see if it's possible.

```
function suggest_out t(user):
   if not user in history:
     return most_popular_this_week()
   else:
      weather, temperature = get_weather_and_temperature_forecast('today')

      if weather == 'sunny' and temperature >= 20:
         if clicked_on(history[user], 'skirts') or count_clicks(history[user]) < 10:
            return out ts_with(weather, temperature, 'skirts')
         else:
             return out ts_without(weather, temperature, 'skirts')
         else if weather != 'sunny' or temperature < 20:
         if clicked_on(history[user], 'jeans') or count_clicks(history[user]) < 10:
            return outfits_with(weather, temperature, 'jeans')
```

```
else:
    return outfits_without(weather, temperature, 'jeans')
else:
    return most_popular_this_week(history[user])
```

5:01 p.m.

I start researching how we can earn money on our app if visitors click to shop or buy things. I had talked to Hailee about it, but never really finalized how to do it. I discover there are special programs that are made for this. I add this to the top of my list to get done right away. First, we really need to figure out how to increase our downloads so we're trending in the App Store.

5:40 p.m.

River texts. The owner of the web domain let it lapse. The site we wanted is now ours!

Almost immediately after, Jack sends me another text asking why I haven't responded about coding club.

ME: I did.

JACK: Oh seriously? I must not have gotten it. Verdict?

ME: I think I'm going to sit this one out.

JACK: Ok. If you ever want to talk about code I'm here.

ME: Yeah, ok.

I keep it vague. I don't want to get into another situation where I'm obsessing over a guy online. Even if this guy is very real.

This is the day in the life of an app developer.

It's also a day in the life of a teenager.

Sunday, October 29

11:15 a.m.

I've been thinking a lot about college and think that I want to major in computer science. Just two short months ago, I had no idea what I wanted to do. It could have been law, medicine, journalism, drama, architecture, science, English literature, engineering, or hospitality. Seriously, I was clueless. But now I know, like really know, I want to get my degree in computer science at MIT.

12:36 p.m.

I'm bored and remember that I haven't been checking The Fashionist's inbox. We probably don't have any messages, but someone should at least be looking at it. To my surprise, there are almost 100 messages—some are spam, some are test messages from River, but there—in big, bold, black letters—are at least 12 complaints. They're so alive with anger they're practically jumping off the page.

Some users are complaining that our SHARE button isn't working properly. Another says that she hasn't seen any new clothing combinations in days. A few users say the app is malfunctioning and not giving them cute stuff to wear from their closets.

Heart drop.

My eyes scan the messages again:

"WHAT THE HECCKKKK?! What am I supposed to do with an app that doesn't work?"

"The app isn't working on my phone! What kind of waste of time is this!!!?????"

"I tried to share this with my friends, but the button isn't even working and then it made my phone freeze. Why would I ever recommend something like this? Bye!"

"This stupid app sucks. Don't get it. Created by amateurs."

"Whoever created this was probably ugly."

I don't look at the screen very long. I don't want the words to settle in. Instead I text Emma and Aisha to declare another emergency meeting.

AISHA: My parents said no because I haven't finished my math homework.

EMMA: Oh shoot, I'm on the Upper East Side at my aunt's. My parents said I can't ditch her dinner.

What am I supposed to do? My heart starts beating—no pounding. I don't think anyone has ever been this mad at me. I've disappointed everyone. This was never my intention. In fact, I wanted to help people with this app, by making them happy with clothing combinations and outfit inspiration. What if they figure out what my name is and try to track me down? Maybe my entire school even hates me now? I'm doomed. I can never leave the house again. Maybe it would have been better if my app had never made it into the App Store. This feels worse than getting turned down.

1:12 p.m.

I think about what to do for a long time, but without Emma and Aisha to bounce ideas off, I decide to show my mom the messages. I mean, what if some furious customer decides to throw a brick through one of the windows of our apartment? She needs to know what's going on ASAP.

"They're just venting, Charlie," she says. "This is a part of running a business and interacting with people. Make sure to address their complaints. That's called customer service, and there's a reason that every company has it—it's necessary."

My mom and I sit down together and come up with a response for each complaint. The bottom line is that I should respond to everyone.

2:21 p.m.

I'm still feeling kind of shaky, so my mom read some of the nice messages we received out loud to me (yeah, there are some not-all-in-caps kind ones, too). One is from a girl in Ohio who found a great outfit for a school party using our inspiration board. Cool! A girl from California said she had a big concert at school but no money to buy a new outfit. She used her combination creator to come up with something fun that she already had in her closet but never thought to wear together.

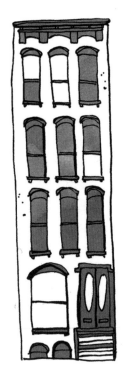

"You've got to take the good with the bad," my mom says.

She's right.

After I get myself calmed down, I realize there are three major problems I need to fix. A few minor things, too, but those will be easy and quick to knock out.

Problem One: The images load too slowly. If this doesn't improve, users will stop using the app. I would, too. I hate it when an app is super slow.

Problem Two: There seems to be a glitch in the code that causes an issue with the correct clothing combinations showing up. Someone looking for an outfit from her closet may get something that doesn't belong to them—or a really ugly pairing.

Problem Three: The SHARE button doesn't work for

everyone. This button is *extremely* important. I want people to share the app on Instagram, Facebook, and Twitter. That's how you get new users.

If I want to do everything properly, it will take me about three weeks. And maybe even longer because I'm not sure how to fix everything. I'm worried that Apple might even throw us out of the App Store when they see how low our rating is right now. I need help. Maybe it's time I expand our team?

Monday, October 30

10:47 a.m.

The assignment in class is to make a list of historical figures to do a long-term study on. But instead, Aisha, Emma, and I are texting our list of potential people to help us get our app back on track. If we just rely on me, it won't be fixed in enough time. We're worried that if the App Store suspends us for even a little bit of time, it opens the door for Dressed to come back. And not to mention, if we start getting competition and other people develop apps like ours, new users will gravitate toward the ones with the best reviews.

Our list:

SAM: He graduated from our school last year but he's in a college not too far away and is studying computer science. Emma added that he has beautiful eyes, but I doubt that's going to improve our ratings, so nope.

QUINN: One of the coding club bros. But Aisha has science class with him and says he's cool.

JACK: Also in the coding club.

ME: How come there aren't any girls on this list? We are The Fashionist—a play on fashion and feminism.

AISHA: There just aren't any.

ME: What about River? She's a girl. She's a coder.

EMMA: She's so full of herself and not friendly. I don't even think she would do it. When she helped us out with coding, she made it clear it was just helping out.

ME: But River is an experienced coder. That's what we need. Not the queen of the popularity club.

AISHA: But so are Jack and Quinn. I know for a fact that Quinn got a 100 percent on his most recent math test. He was talking about it in science.

ME: You don't have to be an ace at math to be good at coding. And this is no joke. Our app is at stake. I just don't know about the boys in the coding club because I already know more than most of them. And Sam's at college now. He probably has different priorities.

I feel panicked. The truth is, I'm hesitant to bring anyone into the circle because I don't trust anyone. But we need to get the app running smoothly.

Amateur. Stupid. Ugly.

The words I use to think about myself stick to me like a stamp.

I take a deep breath. I'm better than that. I'm the boss and I'm taking control.

ME: This is a lot of pressure. This isn't just us playing around with a test version anymore. These bad reviews could ruin everything. I need River. She's the smartest.

AISHA: OK, let's give her a shot.

EMMA: So I don't get a vote? You two just gang up on me and get to decide? River is not a team player. She's so arrogant and is going to blow in here and think that she's just running the show. This is our app.

ME: You don't even really know River, Emma.

EMMA: Oh, really? Do you? Do you know her like you know Seven?

Her comment takes the air right out of me.

AISHA: This pressure is getting to be too much. We need to chill out. We are a team. And Emma, don't forget that River helped us before.

ME: She was download Number 8.

EMMA: Sorry, I was just frustrated. I really shouldn't have said that. Do over! We'll make it work with River.

AISHA: Let's try to talk to her later today.

I should feel better, but I don't exactly. I know that River is already extremely busy with her own app, so I'm not even sure she will be interested in helping us out.

Amateur. Stupid. Ugly.

7:32 p.m.

Nothing is fixed perfectly yet, although I did start fiddling with getting the search function to work correctly. In the meantime, I start to send out the emails to the less-than-happy users.

• • • • • • • • • • • • • • • • • •

Dear RoseFlower,

Thank you for reaching out to The Fashionist. Our customers are of the utmost priority to us, and we're sorry about the issue you're experiencing. We have our developers working on this problem as we speak and will be in touch when everything is fixed.

A huge thank you for downloading and sticking with us through these growing pains.

X

The Fashionist Team

• • • • • • • • • • • • • • • • • •

8:04 p.m.

If starting a tech company seems hard, keeping one going is harder. Maybe my side hustle just should have been a babysitter, like 90 percent of all the girls in my grade. I decide to text Hailee to get her advice.

I sat and thought about what to write for a long time and decided on a version of: Help! Within a minute of hitting send, I already heard back:

> HAILEE: You've built such an amazing team of talent, Charlie! But I think now is the time for you to bring in some more coding power. River? Let me know if you need anything else. –H

I respect Hailee so much, and she thought the same thing I did about hiring River. I do know what I'm talking about and I need to trust my instincts.

I text River, and she agrees to talk with me tomorrow. If she doesn't help, I'm not sure what I'm going to do. Sometimes being the boss is rough.

I'm also staring at the ceiling and thinking about Seven. There's a boy at my school who I imagine looks like him. I don't know why. And the fact I even think about him makes me feel gross.

I go onto the coding forum to see if his account has been activated again. I tell myself it's the very last time. *See it as a sign, Charlie.*

He's not there.

I will never see him on the coding forum again.

But that doesn't mean I will never see him.

That's something I'm about to learn.

The one thing
I learned is,
to just give
everything a
shot. You don't
want to live in
regret.

Chloe Kim

reaching
high

TO DO
TO DOOO
TO DOOOOOO

CITRUS
SUPER C

power
fuel

the
team

#BitterSweet

6:13 a.m.

The sun is still sleeping, but I'm glad that I'm awake.

Amateur. Stupid. Ugly.

The words lit up in fluorescent behind the dark lids of my eyes. I felt locked in with them all night as I tossed and turned in my sleep. But with my eyes open, while the words are still there, at least it's in the context of my room, my phone, my computer, my things—I'm not alone with them.

9:21 a.m.

I'm learning about frogs in the Amazon when I make the decision it's time to talk to River.

"How was your weekend?" I ask.

"Busy," she replies.

It takes me a second to realize that she's talking to me. I have been going over the conversation so many times in my mind—how I would approach River, what I would say, how I would react if she declines the offer I was about to make—that I still felt like I was talking to myself. I recover and respond.

"Oh yeah, me too. A lot of homework?

"No. Just other...stuff," River says.

It gets quiet, the kind you know should be filled with something. River senses it, too.

"Did you want to ask me something? What's up?" she asks.

"My app is breaking and it's breaking me," I say.

The words are out before I can mold and form them into something slightly different and more appealing than they actually are. And less desperate.

"It's all I can think about," I explain. "We're getting complaints about things that aren't working right. I know what I need to do, but I just can't fix everything on my own. I need help, and I was hoping you could officially join our team."

I look down at my gray nails, which suddenly look drab and dull. River's gaze looks equally as bland. She doesn't look excited or annoyed, curious or intrigued. It's impossible to read what she's feeling.

"I'll think about it. Can we talk after school?" she asks.

I nod. Or I say sure. Or I do both. I can't totally remember.

But at least she didn't say no.

3:46 p.m.

I meet up with River near the vending machines. I watch hungry students punch a panel of numbered buttons for their selections. It seems so easy to get what you want. I hope my conversation with River will feel the same.

I show River the complaints and tell her my strategy. To my surprise, she doesn't find the flaws in our app unusual.

"It's pretty common for a first version to have some bugs," she says, as her eyes remain glued to the computer screen and not on me. She clicks, swipes, types. "Overall, I think your approach to fixing all of this is pretty good."

I don't let my fear scare me out of saying what I want to.

"So do you think you can help me get this together?" I ask. "It won't be the same as last time. I mean, this time we'll actually make you a permanent member of the team."

"What does that mean for me? Do I get paid?" River replies.

She asks in a way that makes me feel like her joining The Fashionist is actually a possibility. The fact that I have no money at the moment seems like the smaller hurdle to jump.

"Well, when we figure out how the app can make money, yes," I say. Then I explain the conversation I had with Hailee and how we hope to start incorporating affiliate links.

"Okay, well, I'll think about it," she says. River always has one mode: chill. So I shouldn't be surprised by her answer.

I text Emma and Aisha

ME: There's hope!

It only takes a second for my screen to light up with a text from Emma.

EMMA: You totally flaked on soccer practice today. We need you for the playoffs.

Shoot, I completely forgot about practice. I need Emma to cut me a break. I'm single-handedly trying to salvage our dying app. I'll come up with something later to tell the coach.

9:13 p.m.

Not all is terrible. We just got one positive review for The Fashionist.

"Since I started using this app, I've been able to get ready for school in less than 5 minutes. Game changer! –Lills17"

I want to hug Lills17.

I'm about to send a text to Emma and Aisha telling them about the five-star write-up when a text pops up on my screen.

It's Jack.

Sigh.

JACK: Do you know if we have algebra homework for tomorrow? I had to leave school early today for a dentist appointment and forgot to ask.

I "forgot" to text him back and I "forgot" about soccer practice. Only one of those things are true.

Wednesday, November 1

3:03 p.m.

I force myself to wait all day, but when River doesn't make the first move, I approach her to see if she's made up her mind.

"Not yet," she says.

So I still need to figure that situation out. I also need to figure out how I'm going to study for my Spanish test, finish my science project, and dig into the code to start fixing the app. I can't wait for River to answer.

11:23 p.m.

I lost track of time but am quickly reminded. My mom catches me up and says if I don't do a better job at getting some sleep, she's going to take my computer away. That would be brutal for my business, so I turn my lights out.

Thursday, November 2

6:10 a.m.

Parents get mad if you stay up late, but they don't get mad if you get up early, so here I am—squeezing in a few hours of coding before school.

```
1.    func sayHello(personName: String) -> String {
2.    let greeting = "Hello" + personName + "!"
3.    return greeting
4.    }
```

It feels like I'm going in circles and not truly fixing the problems. Frustrated.

9:20 a.m.

Maybe this is just a symptom of my sleep deprivation, but I have an epiphany. I have been so overwhelmed and full of doom and gloom that I haven't been sure about where to start to fix the app. But the answer is easy, really: The beginning. I have been dipping in and out of too many things. I just need to focus. It's basic, but it's also kind of brilliant.

I hunch over my desk and write out a list. I jot down the main problems and complaints we have right now. I rate them in order of severity and come up with a timeline for how long it will take to fix each one of them. And just like that, I have a plan of attack. I also have a light at the end of the tunnel. Everything will be up and running smoothly in three weeks.

Is it perfect? No. Would I prefer River to join our team? Yes. But for right now, I will start at the beginning.

I also text Emma and Aisha and let them know that we need to update the blog and load more pictures onto the inspiration page—we should pull some from users' personal #OOTD pages, too. We've been lagging on getting up new content, but we need to continue to give users what they love about The Fashionist—the outfits.

Emma: You're back, Charlie!

It sure feels like I am.

Friday, November 3

2:01 p.m.

She's in. River wants to join our team. But there are two things she wants before it's official: for us to get the affiliate links in place within six months so she can start getting paid, and second—and it's a doozy—she wants Jack to join. She'll split half of her earnings with him, so we don't have to pay him extra, but she needs his help to take the app to the level she wants.

River thinks Jack's a solid coder?

I say yes—because I can't say no.

I text Hailee and tell her that it worked—River is going to join the team.

She sends back a thumbs up.

10:17 p.m.

What the...I check the user statistics and there's a huge decrease in new people signing up. This is bad. We need to be growing, doubling, tripling even. But the only thing growing, doubling, and tripling right now is my stress.

I have River to lean on for support, so I reach out to get her take.

After a quick back and forth on texting, we plan to meet up this weekend to start patching up the problems.

Monday, November 6

8:00 a.m.

River and I worked all weekend and we actually got the app to start loading a whole lot faster, and Emma and Aisha posted a new batch of photos. Your move, Monday.

I'm deep in the theory of equations when a text from Emma pops up on my phone.

EMMA: OMG! The Style Tiger is on E! Right now. Turn it on! Turn it on! Turn it on!

I turn my phone over so I can't see the screen. Like I really have time to watch TV right now. I need to finish studying so I can get back to repairing the app.

Once you have a business, it's even more important to take care of it in order for it to grow.

Tuesday, November 7

1:30 p.m.

I haven't been thinking about soccer at all, but I bump into Emma in the hallway and suddenly I have no choice.

"Everyone has been noticing that you're skipping out on soccer practices," Emma says. "Playoffs are this weekend. You need to focus on this."

I sigh. "I'm just really not into soccer. I tried it out for you and to try to find my thing, but I found it now. Can't I just quit?"

"We're so close to the end of the season, you should just finish it out," Emma explains. "I can probably cover for you tonight if you and River plan to work on the app a bit more."

"Please!" She offered, but it still feels like I'm practically begging.

"Yeah, I'll just tell the coach you're sick. But you really need to come to the next practice and, obviously, the game."

"Deal," I say.

4:01 p.m.

I'm at my kitchen table texting back and forth with River about one of the issues users are having when my dad walks in. Normally that would be completely uneventful, but it quickly puts me in panic mode.

"Don't you have soccer practice after school?"

My dad may be a gym teacher, but he never forced me to play sports. However, if I did commit to a team, he has some pretty strict rules about always showing

up, being a good teammate, and never quitting or giving up. Given that my parents have been so concerned about how much time I've been spending on the computer, I need to handle this situation really carefully.

The sky is such a bright shade of blue that I can't blame it on the weather, and he knows my soccer coach personally, so I can't say that practice was suddenly cancelled.

"My hip," I suddenly say. Just like most lies seem to do in my experience, it just sort of falls out of my mouth.

"Your what?"

"You know, my hip." I had complained about it on our trip to Colorado, so it didn't seem like too much of a stretch.

"It's still bugging you?" He looks surprised, as if he's mulling over that something really serious could be wrong.

"Well, it seemed to be getting better but I fell on it during practice this week, and now it seems to be bothering me again." That's the thing about lying. You want it to be quick and almost invisible, like you didn't really do it. But once you tell one lie, you kind of have to keep going, and suddenly they're up to your neck and choking you.

"Stand up and let me take a look."

That's one of the things that sucks when your dad's a gym teacher. He possesses a little more info than most on this kind of stuff. I gingerly stand. I don't want to overreact, but he needs to believe that I'm hurting enough that it would have been impossible for me to make it to practice. I try to distract him.

"I'm not going to let it hold me back, Dad. I'll be at the game this weekend even if I can't play. I want to support my team."

If he acknowledges or appreciates what I'm saying, he doesn't make it clear. "Lift the leg that hurts," he says.

It seems like the smartest plan is to look in pain while I do this. I lift it a bit, wince, and start to wobble. "I don't think I can lift it any higher," I say. "I'm kind of unsteady."

My dad pokes a spot near my hip.

"Ouch," I cry, although not as quick and reactionary as I would have liked.

"You may need to go see a physical therapist. Why don't you keep me posted on how it feels in the next couple of days?"

"Yeah, totally," I reply.

"But you should have gone to practice," Dad says in his kind but scolding voice. "I don't expect you to play, but you can at least be there as moral support for your fellow players."

"It's just so frustrating to have to sit on the bench when all you want to do is play," I say, hoping I sound sincere.

My dad's life mantra in a sentence.

For now, I'm saved.

10:23 a.m.

I keep part of my promise to Emma. I made it to one soccer practice earlier this week, but I just don't have the time to take part in the playoff game today. I never should have signed up for soccer in the first place. I'd rather focus on what I really love—The Fashionist. River and I are so close to crossing everything off the list that needs to be fixed. But getting out of the game will require another favor from Emma.

ME: Before you get upset with me, hear me out. I know I told you I would go to the playoff game, but I can't make it. I need to focus on fixing our app.

EMMA: What? No, Charlie. You've got to be there.

ME: Why? I'm not even a very good player. Me not being there is almost the same as me being there.

EMMA: There's just no way. The coach is going to be furious.

ME: We need to come up with something.

EMMA: What do you mean "we"? And you're coming!

ME: Seriously, Emma. I only ever did soccer for you. I wanted to have something where we could spend time together. I shouldn't be forced to be someone I'm not.

EMMA: You don't have to be something you're not—after the game today. Plus, it's going to be impossible to get out of it. Too much schoolwork isn't an excuse. You already said you're sick and coming up with something more dramatic will cause the coach to reach out to your dad.

ME: Just tell him my stomach flu is back. That the doctor thinks it may be something serious because it appeared again.

EMMA: I don't like this, Charlie. It's a bad idea. But okay. Whatever.

6:44 p.m.

My dad is at the school basketball game with Finn. My mom texts that she's going to a work event and that I should just go ahead and eat without her. I decide to walk to the little café on the corner to grab a quick dinner.

River and I spent the whole day knocking out some of the issues on the app, and I'm mentally going through each strand of code. I'm completely zoned out, when right before I get to the restaurant I accidently bump into someone. I turn to apologize and realize it's Kaia and Roxy, two girls from my soccer team. The problem with that is still fuzzy and out of focus at first, and then Kaia starts talking and it becomes clear.

"Wow, you got better really fast," she says.

"I, uh...," but I struggle to say anything else. I can't seem to form words, only sounds.

"You know we lost because we didn't have enough players," Roxy says. "We actually had to forfeit. What's wrong with you anyway?"

"Nothing's wrong with her," Kaia says snidely. "You should have been at the game today instead of skipping out. It's a real loser move."

Kaia and Roxy aren't known as the nicest girls at school. Over the months I've been playing soccer with them, they've maybe said my name three times. But this isn't them being mean girls. They're telling the truth. I *should* have been at the game. I feel guilty. But I don't know if it's real, or only because I got caught.

Still, I try to salvage the situation.

I wrap my scarf around my mouth and give a little cough even though I know it sounds pretty pathetic and unconvincing. "I'm only out to pick up some soup. It's the only thing I can stomach right now, and no one's home to get it for me." That part sounds a little more convincing.

Neither girl says anything, but as they walk away I hear Roxy say to Kaia, "What kind of stomach flu gives you a cough?"

I should have gone with the hip.

While issues with the app may be clearing up, there's another storm brewing.

Sunday, November 12

12:03 p.m.

Everyone—Emma, Aisha, River, and even Jack—are coming over to my place today. River and I are going to show the fixes we've made to the app. And then we're going to discuss getting the affiliate links in place. Jack's going to help with that.

There's a knock, and it's Emma. She's early.

When I open the door, Emma's face looks like it's holding a secret. Her lips are oddly tight, as if they're doing their best to lock in the words.

Then she lets them out.

"The soccer team is so mad at you."

"Yeah, I bumped into two of them when I was going to get dinner last night," I say, releasing her of the pressure of having to break the bad news that Kaia and Roxy had seen me. "I figured they probably knew I wasn't really sick."

"No, they're like really, really mad." She says it with more emphasis this time. Frustrated that her words are not properly conveying the severity of the situation, she pulls out her phone. She clicks on Facebook and brings up a group page with the name "Charlie Is A Horse." The profile photo is of me, but not truly me. There are illustrations drawn on top of one of my photos to make me look horselike.

"You see?" This time she doesn't speak emphatically, but quietly, as if loud words may shatter my feelings. "Really, really mad."

I don't want to scroll, but I do. The messages inside the group are terrible and mean and viscous. It's mostly pictures of me in my soccer uniform with captions written all over the photos and long strings of comments underneath. Most of the comments focus on my appearance. It's the ones that don't that hurt the most.

"Charlie is a busted liar."

"So she created an app that's kind of dumb and suddenly she is too important to be there for her team."

"If Charlie disappeared from school, I wouldn't even miss her."

"Senior project: What can we do to make Charlie's life miserable?"

"If Charlie got any uglier, it would start falling off and stick to the rest of us. Avoid her at all costs."

"Calling Charlie ugly would actually be a compliment."

"I heard that Charlie got rejected from the coding club because she's not smart enough."

There are more. But I've read enough.

"I'm sorry I had to show you," Emma says, her voice still almost at a whisper. "But I wanted you to hear it from me before anyone else showed it to you."

I'm quiet.

"I can help fix this," she says. "Maybe you can just tell the girls the truth. I think that will help calm things down. If they just understood how much pressure you've been under, it might help them to see that you didn't mean anything by it."

The truth won't work, I think to myself. If Seven told me the truth, it would just confirm to me what a horrible person he really is—not make it easier for me to forgive him. Haven't I been lying to my friends? My soccer team? My teachers? My parents? That is the truth.

"Can we just keep this to ourselves?" The information is public and the whole school probably knows about it, but acting like it's a secret allows me to feel like I have a little control and power over a situation where I really have none. Evidenced by the fact that a new comment pops up:

"All the nasty adjectives you can come up with to describe Charlie. Go..."

"Of course," Emma says. "That's why I came early."

12:30 p.m.
Everyone else arrives, and Aisha's excitement is big enough to hide my feelings. She came up with titles for all of us and is pretty proud of it.

CHARLIE: CEO and Head of App Development
EMMA: Head of Styling and Fashion Partnerships
AISHA: Head of Public Relations
RIVER: Senior Programmer
JACK: Part-Time Senior Programmer

7:13 p.m.
JACK: I saw those comments online about you. And I don't believe any of them.

Embarrassment is the feeling of being exposed. And that's exactly what I am. Burned open by the hurtful words of others. And it won't be long before everyone can see it—the awful guts and inner workings of being me.

I'm not sure how to respond.

JACK: My friend is playing a small concert at a warehouse in Greenpoint. Wanna come? Probably take your mind off that stuff.

So yeah, being exposed is uncomfortable. But the openness allows you to feel kindness like a salve. It feels good. And Jack's words do feel good.

7:17 p.m.
I convince my mom to let me stay out until 10 p.m. on a school night. That never happens. It's either that she trusts me after the situation with Finn—or she just desperately wants me to get out from behind my computer.

I'm standing in a warehouse. Five words I don't know that I've ever said before. I'm with Jack, and much to my surprise, I'm having a good time. It's not like a college party (at least, what I imagine a college party to be like). The space is so giant and open it feels like you're outside. And in the middle of it all, there's a spotlight shining down on a musician playing music that sounds like Ed Sheeran.

Jack is funny and nice—and a part-time drummer.

And the music does, in fact, take my mind off *that* stuff.

Until I go into the bathroom and can't help but check to see if the page still exists. A new post was added four minutes ago:

"Get this! Charlie tried to send me a sext. I blocked her number."

A lie.

It doesn't feel good to be on the other side of one.

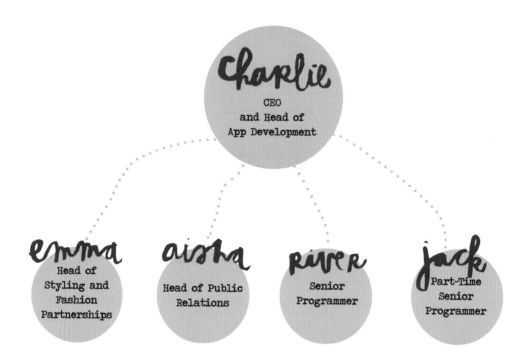

Charlie
CEO
and Head of
App Development

emma
Head of
Styling and
Fashion
Partnerships

aisha
Head of Public
Relations

river
Senior
Programmer

jack
Part-Time
Senior
Programmer

7:11 a.m.

I had the weirdest dream. I was kissing Jack at a party. It must have been Halloween or some type of strange theme party because I was dressed up as a pumpkin spice latte. Jack was wearing a huge fake white beard. I'm not sure exactly what he was supposed to be. But the kiss was terrible and his beard ended up getting stuck in my whipped cream. To make it even more embarrassing, Kaia and Bella were dancing around and making fun of us. They called us rookies and said that we should go back to middle school and learn how to kiss.

Amateur. Stupid. Ugly.

11:04 a.m.

It's awkward being at school. It feels like everyone knows about the secret Facebook group and is staring at me to try to decipher how I feel. It's like, really? You know how I feel. Just imagine if it happened to you. No, seriously, just imagine. Yep, that's exactly how I feel.

1:29 p.m.

Emma and Aisha meet up with me between every period and walk me to my next class.

"This has gone too far," Emma says. "I think we need to tell someone."

"I'm the gossip of the minute, but this too will all go away," I say. "I'm not going to give them the satisfaction of letting them know that I even know the page exists."

"Okay, let's not talk about it then," Aisha says quickly. "We have 43 new downloads."

They drop me off at class and head off in the opposite direction.

While everyone is handing in their homework, I take a second to scroll through Facebook, which feels like the direct opposite of self-care at the moment.

"Let's take bets on how long it takes for her to quit her app."

I know the page exists.

3:00 p.m.

I'm not just imagining that everyone at school is watching me. They are.

I check the Facebook page no less than 22 times. It has 38 new followers, which is more than The Fashionist got today. To scroll through the feed is to get a ridiculous play-by-play of my day:

"Puke. Just walked by the Horse in the hall."

"Horse sighting walking into algebra. You'll probably smell her coming."

"Just a random post to say that Horse does indeed eat like a horse."

5:32 p.m.

I just got home from school and I'm already in bed. I want to hide and never leave this room. My phone is on top of my bedspread and I force myself to leave it there—one click and the tentacles of social media will wriggle into my room and I won't be able to get them to retreat. I tell my dad that my hip is hurting. He totally buys it and says that he's going to make me an appointment to get it checked out with a doctor. I wonder if he can fix a bruised soul and a crushed spirit? That's what I really need.

I make a note in my phone to Google what a sore hip looks and feels like. I need to be prepared for my visit to the doctor.

And then I quickly put down the phone.

Wednesday, November 15

4:32 p.m.

Turns out, you can fake a pretty convincing hip injury just by doing a little bit of searching online.

"Is it a nagging or a stabbing?" My dad set me up with an appointment with Dr. Coles. He's on the younger-ish side and has brown eyes and dark, wavy hair. He looks like McDreamy from *Grey's Anatomy*. I was hoping for a lumpy old doctor. I feel like I'm living my life in a constant state of being flushed, either from lying, blushing, or drooling over my doctor.

"It's a nagging pain, but sometimes it stabs, too. Nagging stabs. You know?"

He asks a few more questions, examines me, and then says he can't find anything majorly wrong.

But.

"Your hip may have been strained too much. This happens to a lot to runners. Do you run a lot?"

"Yes, it's ummm…a form of relaxation for me. I can't get enough of it."

He presses on a few spots around my upper thigh and hip. Each time he asks me if the pressure he's applying hurts. I try to look permanently pained.

"Does it keep you up at night?"

I nod yes.

After he inspects my other leg, he walks over to his desk. 'My guess is that your hip is strained. You need to take a break from running, and soccer, too."

"Do you think you could write a note for me on one of those official papers saying that I'm in need of some rest? My soccer coach can be pretty intense."

He pulls out his prescription pad.

6:45 p.m.

I text Emma a picture of the doctor's note, and she can't even believe it.

EMMA: That letter looks insanely real! How did you get it?

ME: It is real.

EMMA: Okay. Well, it might be time to use it.

She doesn't mention the Facebook group, or Kaia and Bella, by name, but I know what she means.

I scroll to the Facebook group and get a familiar slash of hurt that happens every time I refresh the feed. On the page there is a photo of me, and everyone is taking turns guessing about why I went to the doctor:

"It's obvious, she's pregnant."

You had to have only two brain cells to believe that comment because two posts earlier someone made fun of me for being a kiss virgin.

"She's obviously on drugs. Did you ever notice when she checks anyone's story. It's always crazy late."

"She's the queen of being depressed."

The Internet is wild. I'm using it to build a company, but it's also a tool that's being used to mess with me—first through Seven and now through social media.

3:47 p.m.

Even though the rumors about me being pregnant, depressed, or on drugs are still running rampant through the school, Jack invites me to see another music gig at the Bowery Ballroom. I agree. I even use The Fashionist to help me find a good outfit to wear. I end up in a pair of faux black leather pants, an oversized knit sweater, and black-and-white Stan Smiths.

I delete the Facebook app off my phone.

9:43 p.m.

Jack and I are walking back home from Manhattan across the Brooklyn Bridge—we had to leave the concert early because I told my parents I'd be home by 10. The rows of bridges across the East River look like glow-in-the-dark strands

of pearls. Every now and then our fingers briefly touch or our shoulders rub.

Maybe it was the bare-your-soul music I had just listened to or the cold air literally shaking stuff out of me, but I suddenly felt candidly honest.

"I'm surprised you still wanted to come with me tonight." I'm looking ahead, which makes it feel easier to say.

"Why?" As Jack asks, he seems genuine.

"Because of the rumors. The latest is that I'm pregnant. Hang out with me too long, and you might just become known as the baby daddy around school."

"Forget about those people. They have no lives. You shouldn't even be looking at that page."

I can hear the East River sloshing around below, like a giant puddle. There are ferries, loud tourists, and car horns, even at this time of night. The silence between Jack and me seems just as loud.

"I think I have something that can take your mind off of that," Jack says.

"Like what?"

I've watched enough movies to feel like this may be the lead-in to a kiss. He moves his mouth, but only words come out.

"In coding club today, we learned about the annual Tech&Innovation Awards. It takes place in San Francisco in January. It's kind of like the Oscars or MTV Music Awards—but for tech companies. I know that you're still working the kinks out of The Fashionist, but every year they hand out an award for the most promising start-up. Last year, these two guys won for some sort of DIY-illustrating app they created. I think yours is way better. And I'm not just saying that because I'm technically the part-time senior programmer on staff." He smiles. I couldn't see it in the dark, but I can feel it.

"I've actually always wanted to go to San Francisco," I say. "I asked my parents to take me earlier this year, but there's just no way we stand a chance at that."

"Oh come on, it's at least worth a shot. The winner gets to tour Google's headquarters, gets paired up with a mentor, and wins $100,000 to invest in their company. Seems worth the risk to me."

"The app isn't ready yet. There are still so many bugs."

"Isn't that why you brought River and me on? To handle that stuff?" He's cutting through my excuses with ease, almost as if he prepared for what I was going to say. "I think the guys from the coding club are entering and their stuff isn't nearly as good as yours. If nothing else, do it just to beat them."

Now I'm smiling. I hope he can feel it through the dark.

11:35 p.m.

Earlier I was bummed that I couldn't stay later to hear the band perform their final songs. But after Jack told me about the Tech&Innovation Awards, I couldn't get home fast enough. I grab my laptop and immediately go to their website, drinking up as much information as I can.

They've got so many cool categories: Best in Style, Best in Music, Most Innovative, Best in Medicine, Best in Retail, and The Game Changer. And, of course, the award for Best Newcomer. This prize was created to stimulate young entrepreneurs to work in the world of technology. It's been won before by companies that are now huge.

I go to bed thinking about the possibility of winning the award. I imagine standing on a stage under a spotlight that makes me glow.

8:29 a.m.

A recap of the weekend:

- 72 new downloads of The Fashionist.
- One five-star review
- No negative reviews

After 48 hours of thinking about it, I decide that we should enter ourselves in the competition. We've been frequently updating the app with new content. River and I, along with a little help from Jack, have the affiliate links in place, and there haven't been any major glitches since the first batch. We've told all of our friends, families, and everyone at school. It feels like we're kind of tapped out for new users, and news is spreading slowly. We need to get ourselves out there in a bigger way, and the competition could help us do it.

I bring it up to Emma, Aisha, and River, and they're all for it.

"Sounds like a no-brainer," River says.

"Like we would seriously get to go to San Francisco?" Emma is in disbelief.

"This feels major," Aisha says.

"We probably won't get nominated, but it might at least help connect us with a new base of users," I say as a disclaimer. But I'm secretly excited, too.

We make plans to get together later to fill out the application. There's a bunch of questions we have to answer about our company. They're pretty involved and seem kind of intense, so we decide to all do it together.

First, school.

5:34 p.m.

There are 15 questions on the Tech&Innovation Awards entry form and you also have to complete a press release. It's pretty involved, but it feels good to have a distraction from the Facebook group.

8:02 p.m.

It took almost three hours, but we're done. Aisha wrote up an awesome press release.

NEW APP, **THE FASHIONIST**, HITS THE APP STORE

For those who've always wanted a personal stylist, or even those who haven't, The Fashionist app was released in October of this year.

Billed as a personal stylist you can keep in your pocket, the app was developed by a group of teens from Brooklyn, led by 15-year-old Charlie Wyeth (not a boy). The app uses unique algorithms that allow users to upload their clothes and accessories to create quick, creative fashion looks. The rapidly growing service has recently built on its success and added new features, including a weekly updated blog with style advice, an inspiration board with looks from style influencers, and even affiliate links where users can shop right from the app.

For more information, contact:
Aisha Yahidi
Head of Public Relations
The Fashionist, Inc.
aishayahidi@thefashionist.com

10:13 p.m.
I go through my nightly social media routine.

I keep a few Snapchat streaks alive.

On Instagram, I see Emma posted a picture of us working on the app along with a caption: "Making the dream work."

I barely use Twitter, but do a quick check. Hailee from the Hackathon tagged us in a tweet:

"Tip of the day: Download The Fashionist! I met these girls during the #hackathon. The app is filled with cool and inspiring clothing combinations. It will make your life easier—and chicer. Seriously. Free in the App Store."

Sweet. I snapshot it and send it to our Fashionist group text.

I should end on a high note, but I decide to check to see if the Facebook page is still there. I know I shouldn't read what people are saying about me, but to my surprise, they aren't saying anything at all. The page is gone. In its place is a disclaimer from Facebook: "This page has been removed due to a report that it violated Facebook's terms of service."

Due to a report?

Who reported it?

you don't get what you don't ask for

Emily Weiss

#Spineless

7:12 a.m.

My dreams about kissing a boy have been replaced with dreams of living in San Francisco. The Fashionist had its own office and it looked like something out of a movie. The floors were glittery gold and there was a photo booth.

While I'm dreaming about being an older girlboss, Jack sends me a message and says he wants to talk later at school. He's probably going to come clean about the fact that he's been hanging out with me to get closer to Emma. Seven used me to steal my code, and I'm sure Jack is using me to get closer to my friend. Just another day in the life of Charlie.

11:29 a.m.

Ugh, I bombed a Spanish pop quiz and my grades are seriously suffering. I need to figure out how to get things back on track before report cards come out. If my GPA isn't at least a 3.5, my parents may take my phone, or even my computer, away. That would be a major setback for The Fashionist.

11:31 a.m.

In-between classes, I bump into Aisha and she tells me that Recode Decode, the number one technology-focused podcast that everyone in Silicon Valley listens to, wants to interview us.

This is amazing news! Hailee's tweet has gotten us some serious buzz—a few small tech blogs have reached out to us for interviews—and the app has over 2,000 new downloads!

The problem is that the interview has to happen today. That's in the middle of English and the teacher is tough about missing class. I tell Aisha that I'll make it happen, so now I just need to figure out how to do that.

12:15 p.m.

Jack and I take a walk to get lunch. I'm waiting for his gut punch telling me that he's vibing Emma.

He does make a confession.

It just isn't the one I expect.

"I'm really glad that Facebook page got taken down," he says.

It kind of annoys me. I don't want to be reminded about that dumb page.

"Yeah, me too," I say.

"It bummed me out because I knew it upset you, and..." Jack starts to stumble. "And well, I guess that one of the reasons it upset me so much is because they were talking about someone I really care about. You, I care about you! That sounds like something my grandmother would say. I like you. That's what I want to say."

All I've ever wanted is to hit that high school goal of someone saying that they like me. Shouldn't I feel like I am on Cloud 9? When Jack says it, I don't get butterflies—I get awkward and no one told me that's how it could feel.

Jack keeps talking, which I'm grateful for because I don't know what to say. "I know you're busy with the Tech&Innovation Awards but I thought we could go out on an official date. We've done some stuff together, but I know it was just as friends."

I'm buzzing. No, not literally.

My phone.

I can't help but to glance at my screen—we're walking and Jack doesn't notice. I see that it's because the app has 17 new downloads, which means 17 new people love our app! In the time that Jack has proclaimed his love for me, 17 new people have fallen in love—with our app.

I want to say something riveting and meaningful about how I've always liked Jack, too. But I just don't have the words. I can't tell if it's because I don't feel them or I'm so surprised, I don't know how to express it.

I eventually come up with: "Oh." And somehow that feels huge and monumental to get out, as if I've just delivered the Gettysburg Address. "Let's definitely talk about this after the challenge."

"Yeah, of course," Jack says.

I do appreciate that he isn't being pushy, making me feel guilty for not saying whatever he wants to hear. He's acting like a total nice guy—"a real gentleman" I can imagine my dad saying.

"You're kidding!" I hear Emma's voice before I see her running up to me.

At first, I'm not sure what she's talking about. Jack? The app?

"I can't believe we're going to be interviewed on Recode Decode." Emma just heard about the interview and is doing cartwheels down the school hallway.

"Well, first I have to get permission to do it," I say. River's advice is to just own it.

I walk into the principal's office. My palms are clammy and my nerves feel like they've turned from a private feeling into a public sound. At first, Mr. Mickel says he's busy. He's eating his lunch out of a dingy container as he looks at a stack of papers.

"It's kind of important," I say.

He doesn't exactly look at me, but he does look as if he's listening. "Does this have something to do with the fight that happened after school yesterday?" he asks.

I have no clue what he's talking about. "No, I've actually been asked to do an interview on a technology podcast this afternoon," I say. "It's Recode Decode, actually. I don't know if you've heard of it. I have my own app and they'd like to talk to me about it. I only need about 15 minutes. Well, maybe about 20 minutes. But that's it."

"What is it you're doing?" he asks. Now he's listening. And he motions for me to have a seat in the brown leather chair in front of his desk.

"A podcast interview. For the app I've been working on," I say.

He then begins to ask me a series of questions. Although not the questions I would have necessarily preferred for him to ask me. I would have loved if he asked me about my app. How did I come up with the idea? How did the podcast people find me? How did I get so amazingly smart?

"What class would you have to miss?" he asks.

"English literature," I say.

"How are your grades in English?" he says, pronouncing each syllable slowly.

"Yeah, they're good. I have a C+ but I talked to my teacher, and after my next test I should bump up to a B," I tell him.

The thing is, I'm not even lying. My grades are so all over the place in so many of my classes that an *almost* B does seem like a pretty decent grade.

"Well, for the moment you have a C+, and I don't know that I would call that good," he says. "I think you need to focus on your classes before I let you skip out to talk to some podcast."

"Maybe my grades aren't good, but they are okay," I say, supportively.

"Okay isn't what we strive for at this school," Mr. Mickel declares. "I'm responsible to make sure you're getting the best education you can and also making the most of it. I can't let you miss English when you clearly need to work harder and be in class to learn. Come back to me when you have an A and I'll consider it. The bell's about to ring, so I would get going so you aren't late for your next class."

It's like he isn't taking me seriously because I'm a teenager, but my business is just as real as anyone else's.

Plus, the whole world revolves around technology! Is this guy for real? He doesn't understand and the last time I checked we aren't walking around talking to each other in soliloquies. I am coding. I am preparing for the future. Why is it when you're an athlete you're always allowed to miss class, but I'm not. I have to find a way to do the interview.

I text everyone on The Fashionist team that it's a no-go.

1:07 p.m.

Seriously, they did let me take two full days off to go to Colorado to have fun, but to do something important where I can learn, I get a no? Really?

1:20 p.m.

Options for getting out of English class:

- Faking an illness
- Taking a really long bathroom break and hoping no one walks in
- Skipping class and risking detention
- Lying to the teacher and telling her the principal said I can leave

Nothing looks like a very good option.

And then a genius idea that comes out of nowhere. Well, it actually comes from Aisha in the form of a text on my phone.

AISHA: What about talking to the technology teacher? Maybe he can speak to the principal for us?

Bingo.

1:30 p.m.

The bell rings and we all make a detour to the technology room. River tags along since she's in coding club and has a relationship with Mr. Danson. I explain the situation we're in and show him The Fashionist App.

"Wow, this is really great work, Charlie," he says. "Why aren't you in coding club?"

Major eye-roll.

"I'll talk to the principal and see what I can do. If he gives his approval, I'll come to get you out of class so that you can do your interview. Probably best to do it in this room since no one has class at that time. But I can't make any promises."

The interview is supposed to be at 2 p.m., so I'm a little worried. It doesn't seem like Mr. Danson is going to be able to pull this off. I should have just skipped class. I knew that behind-the-times principal was never going to budge.

My feet tap against the floor and my anxiety is powering me up to make a move. I *cannot* miss out on this opportunity. I'm going to have to go with the super-long bathroom plan.

1:50 p.m.

Mr. Danson walks in the door, and I cannot believe it. He already has River and Jack with him and calls for Emma and Aisha. We all speed walk to the technology room.

One minute early, Aisha dials us into the call. "I have Charlie, lead developer for The Fashionist on the line. Let me know when you're ready for her." After a few seconds, she patches us through to the show.

It was Kara Swisher herself.

"Nice to talk to you, Charlie."

"Thank you," I say. I feel a little breathless, because seriously, this is Kara

Swisher. But I am charged and ready.

"Oh, ha! You're a girl. Awesome. I quickly read your name and was expecting a guy."

"Nope, not a guy."

"Okay, so I downloaded your app and I have a few questions for you."

"Sure."

She then officially introduces me, explains the app, and shares that we're up for a Tech&Innovation Award.

"Tell me about why you decided to create this app."

I look down at my outfit and realize I'm not representing the app very well. I have on a pair of pink leggings, old sneakers, and a gray sweater. But then it hits me—that's exactly why I created The Fashionist. I hadn't used the app today and this was what I ended up wearing. My nervousness evaporates and I begin to share the story of The Fashionist. I explain that I taught myself how to program through various websites and that I also relied on a network of reliable mentors.

Jack gives me a thumbs up.

Emma's smile is nearly swallowing her face.

And I feel like I'm in a groove and my passion for the app is coming through.

I continue the call by sharing what the future looks like for us, especially how we want to begin monetizing the app even more by collaborating with brands we frequently feature.

The interview is moving right along when it suddenly screeches to a halt.

Kara asks where I went to college. My mind goes blank. I start going through the list of colleges in my mind that I'm thinking about applying to in a few years. But I realize that if I lie, the app will lose all credibility.

"Well, I'm thinking about applying to MIT or maybe Stanford. But honestly, I haven't totally thought about it because I'm a sophomore in high school."

Can you cancel a live guest in the middle of a podcast? I'm ready for her to tell me that I'm not qualified to be speaking to her fancy, old audience (not really old but at least older than us!).

"Wow, that is truly amazing. That makes your story even better. It's so great that young women are getting into the field."

Kara ends the interview by giving our app a shout-out, as well as sharing the website where listeners can go to get more information.

"Thanks for the inspiring conversation, Charlie. And let us know how you do with that award."

Just like that it's over. Kara always seems really tough and I think she is, but to us she was nice. They put the podcast up a bit later but they were also livestreaming the interview. We already had 61 new downloads from the time the interview started until it ended, and they're still rolling in. I feel like I could get to the moon on a balloon!

9:24 p.m.
I listen to the interview at least eight times. My voice sounds like I'm talking underwater but whatever, this was a big deal. I can't even believe that our app made it on Recode Decode!

Our app has thousands of downloads, which is right what we needed before the Tech&Innovation Awards announce the finalists.

Wednesday, November 22

9:02 a.m.
The day starts off really good and then I get an email from a local newspaper wanting to profile us. They heard the Recode Decode piece and were impressed that a bunch of local high schoolers were up for a big award in San Francisco. I forward to Aisha to set up a time.

12:59 p.m.
The Fashionist Five are finishing lunch. I'm talking about what a terrible choice I made with the tuna wrap. Emma and Aisha are freaking out over a test they have that afternoon, and River is staring at a breakdown of our analytics. It's in that moment Jack mentions the Tech&Innovation Awards.

"You're not even going to believe this, but my dad told me last night that my stepbrother is entering the competition, too," Jack says. "Apparently his app is really good."

"I didn't even know you had a stepbrother," Aisha says.

"Well, it's kind of a weird situation," Jack explains. "He's not exactly a stepbrother because my dad is no longer dating his mom—it's her kid with another dad. But my dad still talks to him and still treats him like a member of the family. He lives in Connecticut so we don't see him very much. I just thought it was so random."

I'm only half listening. Our app is blowing up—in a good way this time—so I don't really care about Jack's stepbrother-no-brother's app. I'm sure a lot of talented people are entering the competition. But I'm not focusing on that.

"What does his app do?" River asks. Of course River is interested in sizing up the competition.

"Well, the weird thing is it's sort of similar to ours. He also allows people to put together outfits from their closets. I know it seems strange, but I guess it's kind of like Snapchat and Instagram. Once one company does something and it's successful there's sort of a trend in similar technologies. My dad said he's been building it for a while but there were issues with getting it into the App Store. I guess he made the corrections and it's good now."

My ears perk up. An app like ours? Problems with the App Store? It seems eerily familiar. I'm nervous to ask the next question, but I know I have to.

"What's the name of the app, Jack?"

"I think it's called ClothesHanger."

I feel relieved. It isn't Dressed.

"We should probably check it out just to make sure ours truly is the dominant one of the two products," River says. "It's not unusual for there to be similar apps, but we need to cover our bases. Is it in the App Store yet?

"I can even do a little digging and talk to Seven myself," Jack says.

Puke boils in my stomach and up to my throat.

"Who?" Emma is wide-eyed.

"Oh yeah, I know, weird name," Jack says, clueless. "Everyone calls him by his last name for some reason. But his name is Theo."

It's a name we all know.

He's back.

there
is no limit
to what we,
as women,
can
accomplish

Michelle Obama

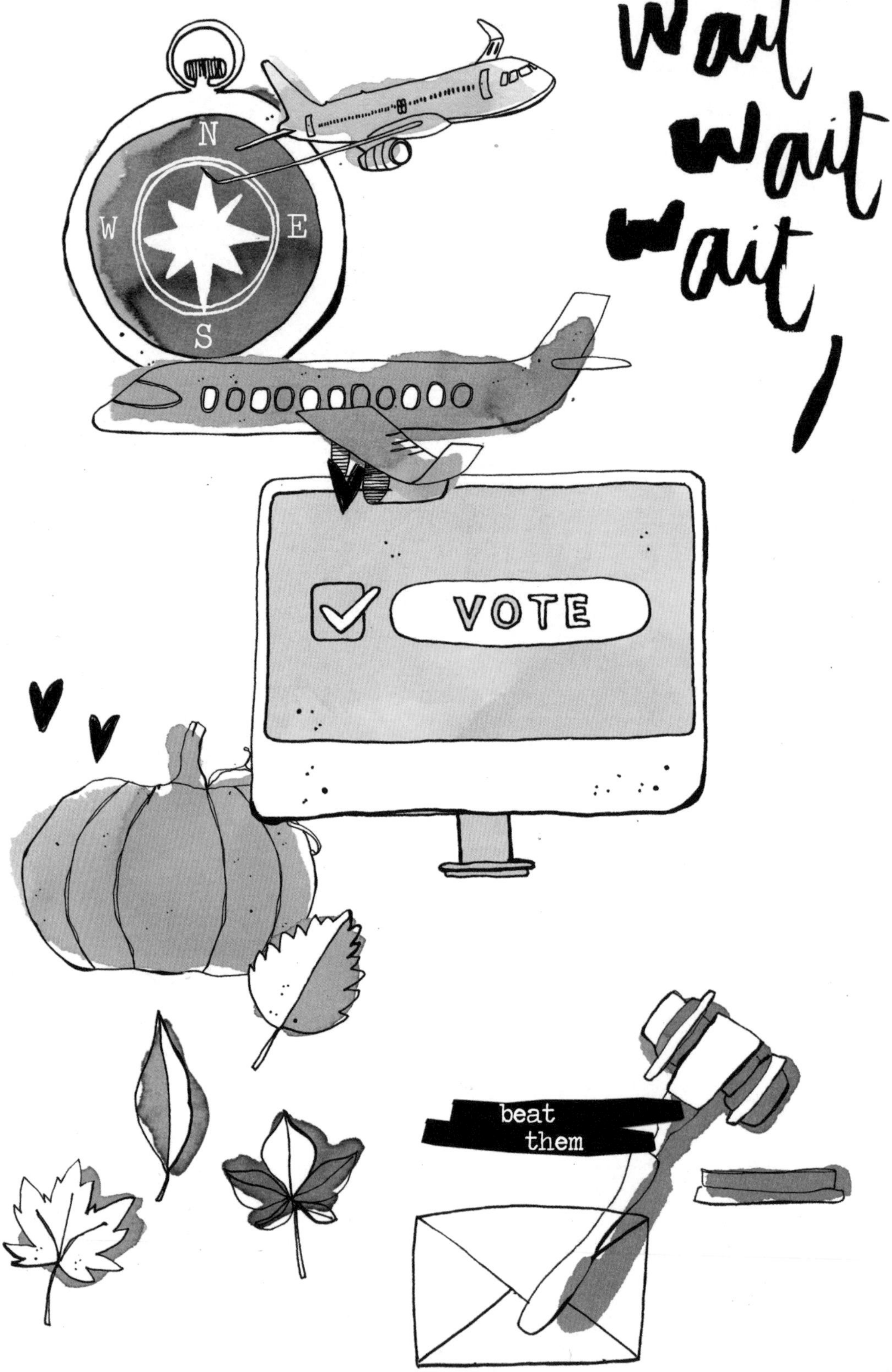
wait
wait
wait
N
W
E
S
VOTE
beat
them

#Independent

3:03 p.m.

The minute the bell rings, we huddle around our phones, looking up ClothesHanger.

It seems that Seven is as shameless as ever. The app is almost a carbon copy of ours. Apparently after he got in trouble, he just made some small tweaks to his code, changed the name to ClothesHanger, and released it again on the App Store. There isn't much we can do. Having your idea cloned is devastating, but not illegal.

River is ready to wage a battle. "Why don't we clone some of the new features that he added in? Two can play this game."

"Let's not stoop to his level," Emma says.

8:33 p.m.

We just had our Recode Decode interview and our downloads since then have been impressive! We almost hit 10,000 today. But there's only one number I can focus on: Seven.

10:09 p.m.

I really need to get some sleep. It is Thanksgiving tomorrow. I love Thanksgiving. I love the time with family, the food, the way the city looks, happy people walking around. First I was a bit torn since there is so much work to do on the app but then I decided that will always be the case, and relaxing is important, too. Hello, self-care! I am also hanging out with Emma this weekend and we agreed we are just going to hang out and have fun.

Monday, November 27

6:15 a.m.

All I know is that the Tech&Innovation Awards nominees will be announced around the 27th "depending on the number of entries." Apparently that does not mean

November 27th at 6:15 a.m. After doing a quick search, nothing has been posted. I am hitting the snooze button on my phone to try and sneak in a little more sleep.

7:33 a.m.

My mom is on a breakfast kick and is making kale-and-tomato-egg bites.

"Grab a couple to take with you," she says.

"I'm already full."

"Full? Of what? You just got up."

Fair question since I just walked into the kitchen.

I want to say that I am full—of nerves. But instead I grab a few egg bites and then head out the door.

8:15 a.m.

As I walk into school, I check the Tech&Innovation Awards site and social handles again. Not a mention of the nominees anywhere. I also look to see if anyone's tagged Tech&Innovation—just in case someone leaked it online. Nothing. Nothing under any related hashtags either. I don't know what's driving me more to find out—my own excitement about being in the running or the anxiety of knowing that Seven potentially is, too.

12:00 p.m.

As soon as my phone turns to 12:00 p.m., I refresh everything. It's officially work hours on the West Coast, and I imagine they'll get the news out first thing.

Nope.

Plus one for impatience.

2:15 p.m.

We have to come up with a short story in English literature class. I name mine: "San Francisco Is Keeping a Secret." Mrs. Hobes said, "It's a story she'd like to read."

5:25 p.m.

A question mark from Emma pops up in the group text. It's probably the hundredth time someone—Emma, Aisha, River, or Jack—has checked in about the awards. We're all on edge.

7:23 p.m.

It doesn't look like we're going to hear anything today. It's almost the end of the day in San Francisco.

Jack texts me.

JACK: Don't worry! We'll get good news.

It reminds me that I still have to talk to Jack about what he brought up the other night.

9:06 p.m.

I keep replaying the podcast interview in my head. It might not have been great timing for us to do that. Clearly the judges must have listened to it and weren't impressed.

Tuesday, November 28

9:02 a.m.

Waiting does terrible things to you, which is my way of saying—it was a long weekend.

12:29 p.m.

It's Pizza Friday—on a Tuesday—in the cafeteria.

I'm debating between a cheese or veggie slice. I hear a ding from my phone. Email. I had decided to check in with Hailee about the reappearance of Seven to see if it happened to be some sort of violation, and I hope it's her emailing me back with good news:

Dear The Fashionist Team:

Thank you so much for your Tech&Innovation Awards application. Competition this year was our fiercest yet, which while we are glad to see, we're also sad that we cannot extend an invitation to everyone to compete.

However, we are very pleased to inform you that your app, The Fashionist, was impressive and we would be happy to extend an opportunity for you and your team to join us as a finalist at the Tech&Innovation Awards. They will take place this January in San Francisco. Upon acceptance of your attendance, we will send along additional details.

We look forward to meeting you in person.
Best,
The Tech&Innovation Awards Judges

● ●

It's better than good news. It's the best news.
I'm about to tell everyone, but I don't have to.
"That face," Emma exclaims. "We're in, aren't we?"
"We're in."

2:56 p.m.

The smiles still haven't left our faces. The news feels as good as I thought it would. I don't know what being popular is like (although our app is trending in the App Store—does that count?), but being recognized for the thing that makes you, well, you, is so amazing. This isn't just a fluke appearance on a podcast, or an interview with our small newspaper, or impressing the technology teacher at school—we're being recognized by some of the most brilliant minds in technology.

There's only one thing that would make this better: If Seven doesn't make the cut. But we don't say that part out loud.

5:23 p.m.

We're all on our group text. After officially accepting our spot, we discovered there's a catch: Only the top three apps will travel to San Francisco for the chance to be crowned the winner. And from the pool of candidates that the awards committee nominated, the top three are determined by a public vote. The judges believe that the enthusiasm of an app's fan base should be a factor when determining who the true standouts are.

We need to figure out how to get the word out to our user base about voting. Voting closes in mid-December so we have just a few weeks, which seems like a lot of time when you're studying for a test or writing a term paper, but not nearly enough time when you're trying to be crowned the queen of new apps.

"This should not be a popularity contest," River says. "I mean, what a ridiculous process. And all of these tech geniuses will probably just code bots to vote for them."

I can always count on River to keep it real.

7:03 p.m.

When my mom walks in the door from work, she's carrying a bunch of lilies. They're for me.

"I'm so proud of you," she says. "So smart and kind and brave."

Smart. Kind. Brave.

I like the sound of that.

Wednesday, November 29

8:41 a.m.

News of our nomination has spread through school. So many students congratulate me I don't even know all their names. My locker feels like the first pit stop everyone makes before continuing on with their day. Apparently, Miss Popularity (do I really need to clarify that's Emma?) is already telling everyone about voting. There is even a committee of people at school advocating for votes for us! The school's Facebook page put up a message, the senior class president spread the word during the morning announcements, and the school's student government is planning to cover the neighborhood with flyers and posters. Aisha also reached out to the newspaper reporter who wrote that article about us and had them do a little update to their piece. And Hailee sent me a text that she was so amazed by what we were accomplishing.

When I got the email that we had been accepted, it felt like I had been given a piece of the world. Better even—that I created a piece of it. And I feel like I've been floating ever since. I did this. Me.

Amateur. Stupid. Ugly.
Smart. Kind. Brave.
I try to shake it off.

9:47 p.m.

There's been an elephant in the room (is that the correct expression?!), and River finally says what we've all been thinking.

RIVER: You haven't heard from Seven, Jack? You haven't asked him or talked to your dad about his app?

JACK: No. We honestly don't really talk. My dad said that he forgot to ask Seven about it the last time they talked.

AISHA: That seems like good news for us then, right? I mean, wouldn't he have brought it up if he had been nominated?

ME: You know what? We haven't even gone online to see if there is some sort of announcement! They could have put it on Twitter or even on their website.

Nobody responds. Probably because our fingers are too busy searching online. It only takes 30 seconds to get our answer: There is a full list posted on the Tech&Innovation Awards website. It's kind of embarrassing that it took us this long to check it out.

The first thing I see is our spot—we're Number Eight. My eyes immediately wander to spot Number Seven because, of course, he would be there. That's just how the Universe has been working lately. But no. It's a company called Wendy that developed some sort of robotic cleaning service. My eyes keep looking. The Fashionist, Wendy, Ace, Served—ClothesHanger. He's at spot Number Six. I'm not sure what it means that he's listed sixth, and we are eighth.

Thursday, November 30

11:21 a.m.

Well, we know. But there's nothing we can do it about it. Hailee had already responded a few days ago that since he rectified the problem Apple cited him for and changed the code, he can't be penalized for something he's already been punished for.

To boost the mood, or at least to boost my mood since he only sends texts to me, Jack texts some links. The Fashionist is mentioned in a few tech newsletters for our nomination, and Recode calls us a "promising app" after our podcast aired.

Sometimes it seems Jack feels guilty for the actions of Seven. I'm not even sure why. They aren't really brothers and they basically never talk to each other and maybe only see each other once a month.

12:38 p.m.

Jack's on a school field trip for the rest of the day, so when I see River, Emma, and Aisha, I show them the articles that he sent me.

Emma, always the hawk, notices that the links are in a text stream that's really long. "It looks like you and Jack talk a lot outside of The Fashionist group text. How often do you both talk to each other?"

"Well, I don't know. I'm not exactly counting." I regret how it comes out— defensive and borderline rude. "He just reaches out about homework and stuff like that."

"Okay, right, Charlie. Come on, tell me the truth."

"Alright," I say. But a confirmation of the truth just won't cut it. They want the full truth. "We used to talk quite a bit actually."

"You used to, or you do?" Emma isn't dropping it.

"We were talking about the app and homework and stuff every now and then. It really wasn't very much. But then we did start talking more because we were hanging out sometimes. We saw some concerts together. He knew I was taking everything that happened with the Facebook group really hard. But I've been so focused on the Tech&Innovation Awards that we really haven't talked much outside of our group texts."

It must have been enough because Emma drops it.

Instead, we hop on our phones to look more closely into whom we're up against. There are some pretty awesome projects. One company developed LED-technology that could be put into clothes so they suddenly shimmer or light up—like KiraKira+ in real life. Another team we really like call themselves Tauble. It stands for tech plus baubles. They created a line of fashion wearables. It's sort of like an Apple Watch on steroids. A few other ideas and apps catch our eyes, but they seem to have small user bases, which hopefully means they may not be able to come up with enough votes.

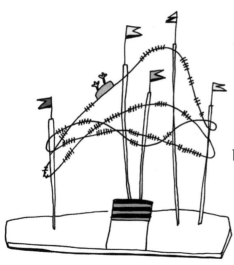

7:55 p.m.

We plan to get together this weekend to do a little editorial planning for the app. With the holidays coming up, we want the outfit inspiration posts to be really strong. People may be coming for our business, but we're not giving up and will continue to work hard on *our* idea.

In the meantime, Jack is texting me, asking if my English lit teacher also gave me a deadline of Monday for the reading assignment that's due. I see that he has a new profile picture. He looks super cute. His shirt sleeves are perfectly rolled up, and he's sort of smiling in a way that feels candid. Why do rolled-up shirt sleeves make a guy look hotter?

I have been waiting my whole high school life for a moment like this. In fact, I've been trained to believe that when a guy gives me attention, I've done something right. And that's exactly what's happening. It does feel good to have Jack think I'm special enough that he wants to take it to the next-level, but it also feels weird. Weird because I don't like Jack. I mean, I do like Jack—just not like that. I wish someone would have told me that sometimes when someone gives you special attention, you might have to tell them to keep it.

8:40 p.m.

Jack is still texting me, but it's moved from straightforward homework talk on text to flirty messages on Snapchat. Maybe they're not even flirty. I don't know. He keeps sending selfies with filters on them. I respond to the first couple, but what is there to say about Selfie No. 17?

I log on to the app administrator page to see what people have been saying recently about The Fashionist instead.

10:52 p.m.

Maybe it was rude of me not to respond to Jack?

I decide I need Emma's advice. She always has the best relationship advice. Sounds like the beginning of another app.

10:40 a.m.

Jack texts me to hang out later.

I text Emma to see what I should do:

Me: So I think Jack likes me. Actually, I know he does because he told me.

Emma: I could so totally tell! I'm smiling for you.

Me: This is where I need your advice, though. I don't really like Jack like that. It's not even Jack. I think Jack is cool and cute and has awesome taste in music. I just don't want a boyfriend at all. What is wrong with me?

Emma: What? Why would something be wrong with you. You do not need to be in a relationship to be happy. You just do you.

I feel so much better. Now I just need to figure out how I'm going to break the news to Jack. I start to get nervous. What if Jack gets so mad at me that he tells Seven everything about our new app features? I forgot to mention it before, but Urban Outfitters reached out to us to create a special collection—and we really need to keep that under wraps.

It all happened because one of the store's executives started to use the app, and she really loved it. She talked to her bosses and thought it would be great for us to partner up and sell a special capsule collection for our app's users. But there are a lot of corporate hoops to jump through before anything is official. And then if we make it to San Francisco, that news will be our secret weapon to really stand out and show the dynamic ways we're growing. That's a lot of *ifs*, though. So far, it's just been a lot of emails going back and forth—probably about 50 just to set up a meeting.

But it goes to show that if you're original and work hard, people take notice. Even if nothing comes out of it, I love that people in fashion are seeing and loving what we're doing.

I feel like Jack is a good person and wouldn't do anything like that. But there was a time when I thought Seven was a good person, too. I need to be more tentative when trusting people.

1:04 p.m.

I decide it's now or never. I don't want to get back to school after holiday break and not have talked to Jack. I text him that we should talk.

Jack sends me a picture of a new Mexican restaurant that opened up a block away from me. He suggests we meet there because they have some sort of cactus juice that everyone is posting on Instagram.

The plan is in motion.

But now I feel paranoid. Maybe I'm just completely overthinking this whole thing. Just because Jack said he likes me doesn't mean that he wants to be exclusive. He never asked me to officially be his girlfriend. And he sent that text so many days ago. Maybe he doesn't even feel that way anymore. Since then, here's what he's said to me:

- "Is your homework also due on Monday?"
- "Is today pizza day in the caf?"
- "Did you know that Mrs. Hobes is out today?"

Here's what he hasn't said:

- "You are so hot."
- "Your smile is the only thing I want to see in this world."
- "Be my girlfriend?"

Nothing like that. I'm a complete relationship rookie.

1:32 p.m.

It might be because I'm stressing about meeting up with Jack, but I do something I haven't done in a long time: I go on to the coding forum to see what Seven has been up to—whom he's been helping, what he's been saying on the community board, and if he's shared any info about our app.

I immediately regret it and click off the page.

I do something more constructive to deal with my nerves instead: I open up my coding program. When I'm writing code, it's like I'm rewriting my feelings. I feel connected to what I love and it always makes me feel better. There's something really therapeutic about sitting with my computer creating things with 0s and 1s—not scrolling through social media, worrying what other people are thinking about me or thinking about all the schoolwork I have to do.

Self-care.

Progress.

Jack and I meet up and both agree the cactus juice is overrated. It does look cute on my feed though.

I know I just need one good word to get the conversation with Jack started, but it feels impossible to dump someone you aren't even dating. The Pre-Dump. Is that even a thing?

Jack beats me to the punch.

"I'm actually really glad that we could meet up because I've been dying to talk to you. I want to come clean about something that's been eating away at me. When you tried to get into the coding club, I started following you on social media and got a crush on you. I loved how uninterested you were in all the dumb high school drama. It was really refreshing. But I didn't know how to talk to you. Since you were into technology, but didn't get into the coding club, I figured you might be on that online tech forum. I know a lot of programmers at school use it. I figured the chances were slim but I thought if I could get even just a little info about you, I might have something to start a conversation with. My dad had dragged me along to Seven's house one night and we were bored and sitting around, so I asked him if he could help me find you. Unfortunately, he did, and basically tried to ruin your life. And it's all my fault."

News flash of the day: Boys are just as insecure as girls.

"But listen, I honestly had no idea what Seven was doing or that he would steal your app idea. He actually told me that he had found you, but that you never responded to his message. Little did I know, he was actually prying you for information."

Jack cast his eyes down, and it makes me feel bad. I know what it's like to be tricked and deceived by Seven. We have that in common.

"Gosh, Jack. Wow. I was not expecting that at all." I process, debate, and decide how to proceed. "I believe you. I know how Seven can be. He lied to me, too."

"No hard feelings for real?"

"No hard feelings for real," I confirm. "But since we're being honest, there's something I need to talk to you about, too." The weight that had just lifted off Jack's shoulders appears to have returned. His face looks worried. "I really love being your friend. In fact, you are actually one of my best friends. But I'm really not looking to date anyone right now. I'm just really happy. I love the way that things are going with the app right now and with my friendships, too. Everything just feels so good and I feel so complete that I don't want to change that."

I don't overexplain it or try to fill the silence with hollow words. That's it. The truth. I'm not sure how I expected Jack to take it. Maybe he would get angry at me, maybe he would get up and leave so quickly he'd spill our electric-green cactus juice all over me, or maybe he would say, "What are you talking about, Charlie?"

But instead:

"I get it. I really appreciate you being honest, but I would be lying if I said I'm not bummed. But it's hard to be sad when I have you as a friend. And for being so cool about the situation with Seven."

"We're good, then?"

"We're all good."

And then I drop a giant hunk of creamy avocado on my shirt. Smooth, Charlie. Smooth.

Sunday, December 3

11:13 a.m.

Today is all about the app life, which is the best life. River and I work on adding the ability for users to vote for us in the Tech&Innovation Awards right from the home screen on the app. With over 3,000 new users in the past couple of weeks, this should definitely give us a competitive edge. My new mantra is to focus on my business, run my own race, and not pay attention to anyone else.

Monday, December 4

8:28 a.m.

I see Jack right before homeroom and he gives me a half smile and keeps going. I begin to wonder if he didn't take the news so well and is going to reach back out to Seven and plot the ultimate revenge on me. But I don't even let myself go down that train of thought. It's not about trusting Jack or Seven—I need to learn to trust myself. I did the right thing.

9:45 a.m.

My phone beeps in the middle of class, and I try to hide it under my desk before the teacher hears it. But I can see enough of the screen to know that River made it happen. The push notifications to encourage users to vote are being sent. It's time for people to start voting. We'll just have to see how this goes.

I stack up a pile of books on my desk to hide my phone and begin a group text with Emma, Aisha, River, and Jack:

ME: Is there any way for us to see how many people voted?

AISHA: I don't think so.

RIVER: No. At least not legally, anyway.

The thing about group texting is that there's so many different thoughts going on at the same time, and this one is no exception.

EMMA: How much do you talk to Seven about tech stuff, Jack? I'm worried he's going to hack into your computer or something next time he's around.

No response from Jack. But he hasn't said anything so far, so maybe he's just not available. After all, we are supposed to be focused on class right now. Emma follows up with a question mark.

JACK: I'm here. Sorry. My teacher is super strict about no phones in class.

Aisha sends a smiley emoji to lighten the mood.

JACK: We don't really talk that much since the parents split. I'm keeping my distance and will definitely be keeping my computer at a distance.

RIVER: Well, if you do get any information about what he's working on, let us know.

JACK: We really aren't that close anymore. Seriously. But OK.

EMMA: We don't want to play by his shady rules anyway. We can legitimately win this on our own.

AISHA: Exactly!

As we're all talking, Emma is side texting me to find out if I've talked to Jack yet.

ME: Yep, it's all good.

EMMA: Seriously?! It's time for a catch-up sesh!

1:12 p.m.

I schedule another round of texts to go up on all of our social media channels reminding our users to vote. I really wish we could have some insight into how it's going.

2:56 p.m.

I'm getting anxious to hear who made the finalist spots. I look up fun restaurants to visit in San Francisco. So far I have:

- Marlowe
- Hawker Fare
- La Taqueria

4:00 p.m.

My mind is off of Jack, Seven, the app, and whether we're going to actually make the finals. This week is the #hourofcode—a worldwide movement that inspires millions of students to learn coding. The organization offers a bunch of classes that you can do within an hour. I am going to participate. I take one of the challenging ones and focus. The clack of my keys, lines of beautiful code on the screen—my happy place.

Everyone has something they love, and for me, this is it. I can open up my computer and create something out of nothing. It could be something fun or it could be something that changes the world. There are no limits to code—you can be and create whatever you want.

Tuesday, December 5

7:23 a.m.

I need to come up with my speech in case we win. I read once that the shower is a great place to come up with creative thoughts, so I try it out while washing my hair. It smells like fresh-cut flowers and the sun.

"I would like to thank everyone who made this possible, especially our killer team at The Fashionist. We have dealt with people who wanted to steal our ideas and our code, others who doubted us, and haters all along the way. But here we are—victorious!"

Wow, that's a really terrible speech. I need to work on what I'm going to say—somewhere else besides the shower.

1:14 p.m.

In biology and I'm bored. So bored.

I'm getting everything ready for The Fashionist team to come over to work on our app—just like the good old days before we were worried about awards. River, Jack, and I are cleaning up some code while Aisha and Emma work on new fashion editorial content. That's when I see it: an email from Urban Outfitters.

. . . .

Hi The Fashionist Team:

We hope this email finds you well. We're sorry for the delay in getting back to you. After our discussions regarding a fashion-line partnership, we have decided that we would love to forge ahead with your team. The next step will be for each of our style teams to collaborate on a few key pieces, and then our programming teams will get all of the stuff on the back end working. We really look forward to working on this exciting launch together!

XX

Urban Outfitters Team

. . . .

This is unbelievable! My jaw is on the floor. Is this real life? What started as an idea to do something fun with technology has turned into a successful app and even a clothing line. I cannot believe we're going to have our own exclusive line with Urban Outfitters. Hello world!

I tell everyone about the email and how the deal is official. The only way to describe what happens next is: Everyone basically lost their minds.

Me: Should I respond right away?

Aisha: Probably not. We'll look thirsty. Tomorrow morning?

We all go back and forth for a bit trying to decide. Aisha and Jack are unsure— they think it might be best to hold off. Emma, and surprisingly River, say we should ink this thing right away before the next big app shows up on the scene.

Forget the rules, I think. I tap out an email right away letting them know we're bursting with excitement. They forget the rules, too, and respond back almost immediately with a time to meet next week. The awards seem far off and untouchable, but this seems real—like I could reach out and grab it. Or at least take the A train to it.

5:03 p.m.

I'm scrolling through social media while my dad finishes making dinner. I see a promoted post: "Check out the app ClothesHanger so you can be out the door in the morning in less than 10 minutes."

My first reaction isn't to feel down and wallow in self-pity—it's to rally our team. I am the leader of our group and I want to act like one—to act like a boss.

I send out a group text to the team:

Whatever happens with the voting, we are already winners! Look at all the people using our app—we've helped them feel happier and better about themselves. That's pretty freaking amazing! Oh, and did I mention we have a clothing line with Urban Outfitters?

I follow it up with a string of prayer-hand emojis.

Friday, December 8

3:00 p.m.

Today will be the last day people can vote! Now we have to wait for the news. But first, some bad news in the form of an email:

Dear Miss Wyeth:

I am emailing you on behalf of my client, My Celebrity Closet. It appears that your app, The Fashionist, is in direct competition and infringes on the code and intellectual property of my client. To prevent further legal action, we demand that you remove your app from the App Store immediately. If this does not happen within 48 hours, we will have no choice but to pursue this matter in court, where you will be subjected to a lengthy process that will end with you not only paying a civil penalty but also my client's legal fees.

We appreciate your cooperation in this matter.

Sincerely,

Mark Pithon

General Counsel | Pithon, Pittman, and Barnes

We're done.

I
kinda
like the
idea of
being
scared

Selena Gomez

sparkle like crazy

best time
of the
year

#Imposter

6:55 a.m.

It was the weekend from, well, you know. After talking to everyone about the potential lawsuit, we all decide that I have no choice but to tell to my parents about the email. It seems like a pretty serious matter. Emma is convinced we might even go to jail.

So when my alarm goes off this morning, it isn't really functioning as an alarm clock, but more of a reminder as to how long I've been awake and wide-eyed—a ringing finish line to a long night of tossing and turning. Some questions I tried to figure out the answers to under the tired glow of the moon:

- Would we have to hire an attorney?
- How much would that cost?
- Would we need to take down our app?
- What does that mean for our line with Urban Outfitters?
- Could we just tweak our app to be slightly different?
- How did we miss this?

7:57 a.m.

I talk to my parents before leaving for school. My mom says she'll think about what we should do and will let me know. My dad is adamant that whatever it is needs to involve an attorney. I feel better knowing that they'll handle it. But when I get to school and think about how they had only said the words necessary and not much else, that's when I realize my parents are really scared and worried, too.

10:31 a.m.

I got a text from my mom letting me know that she discussed our situation this morning with Rabia Hewitt, an attorney (Mom, FTW!), and that she requested to see all of the information. Within an hour, she had already looked it over and called my mom back to set up a meeting at our apartment tomorrow after school to discuss how we should proceed. I should be happy that my mom is being such a rockstar and taking care of this, but all I can think is: Another full day of waiting. Almost two, really.

Not everyone is freaking out as badly as I am. Emma, yes, and Aisha a little bit, too. But Jack and River aren't really worried at all. They understand the code and say there's absolutely nothing to worry about. River found the app but it really does not look special at all and the features don't even look like ours.

To add to the unfortunate timing, we have our meeting with Urban Outfitters today. It seems like a waste of time and I want to cancel, but Jack persuades me that we should go and that we shouldn't say anything about the legal situation yet.

"It's nothing more than an email at this point—it's not even real," he says.

As the boss, I know we have to persist, so I decide to keep the meeting.

Not every day is going to be a good one when you're running a business—it's impossible—but you have to keep working and can't give up.

3:14 p.m.

We're on the train into Manhattan. Urban Outfitters has its headquarters in Chelsea. I'm feeling annoyed at everything—especially the guy who keeps hitting me with his backpack (doesn't he know you're supposed to take those off on crowded trains?)—and even a little bit at the little old lady sitting in the corner of the train knitting what looks like a scarf long enough to fit around the neck of a giraffe (why do people do personal things in public places?).

My bad mood is big enough that it's bumping into everyone around me.

"Stop being so extra, Charlie," Jack says.

But that just makes me feel worse. I want to scream at him that he's just being nitpicky because I wasn't interested in going out with him. But somehow I refrain. I feel embarrassed by the idea of getting into a screaming match in front of the old woman with such white powdery hair. She reminds me of my grandmother. And then I feel guilty for being so annoyed with her.

But in this moment, rocketing under the East River, I feel overwhelmed—like the entire weight of the city is resting on my shoulders. And in that minute, while I'm underground, I guess it kind of is. I'm responsible for this app—it's going to help me get into college, allow me to pursue my passion in the tech industry, help people solve a problem, and maybe even make my friends and me some money. But I'm letting everyone down by getting us into another mess. I should have done deeper research on the competition.

3:58 p.m.

We walk into the lobby at Urban Outfitters, and everything feels so professional and legit. It feels like we don't belong. We're used to working out of someone's bedroom. I forgot to even put moisturizer on my face this morning. Jack's hair looks a little sloppy—not in an effortlessly messy way—but in a way that it looks like he just hasn't brushed it. Emma's black boots look worn and scuffed. Aisha and River are dressed like they're going to school for the day (which yes, I guess we all did just come from class). What were we thinking? I guess the problem is that we didn't.

"So you're all with The Fashionist, right?" The receptionist motions us toward a closed door before we even give an answer.

Hearing the name of the app I built gives me both a burst of satisfaction and a pang of torment because it feels like we might lose it all. This is everything that's going on in my head right now, but for the time being, there can only be one thing: this meeting.

"Yes, we're here with The Fashionist."

I say it firmly, even if my jitters are back—and all the restless butterflies they bring with them.

5:20 p.m.

The meeting is flying by. It's so much fun, it doesn't even feel like work. It isn't a scary boardroom situation. We're all in a room with a few people from Urban Outfitters. There is a conference table, but there is also a circle of bean bags and that's where we all meet. One girl has a giant lion tattoo going up her arm, so suddenly my varsity jacket, Jack's hair, Emma's boots—not even a thing.

We walk them through the app a little bit more and how the announcement of the clothing collection, as well as the ability to buy the items, will be incorporated into the interface. River fires off some great ideas and the executives look interested—they type most of what she says into their laptops. They give us a tour of their design department and introduce us to Beenie and Leta, the lead designers, whom Emma and Aisha will be working with. We go through a very detailed list of next steps that we all feel good about.

It's happening!

Some may think a tech job is sitting in a basement, but it's not—some days it's writing code like you would write a book on a computer and other days it's floating around fashionable offices in the middle of New York City, talking about how to bring style to people in fun and unique ways. That's tech, too. It's anything and everything.

The lawsuit (or potential lawsuit) might as well have been something that was happening to somebody else. Because for the entire meeting, I don't even think of it. Not even once. I don't think Emma, Aisha, River, or Jack do, either.

But once we're done and get closer and closer to Brooklyn and farther and farther away from those dope offices in Manhattan, it feels like not only has the lawsuit reappeared—it's also looming even bigger. If the developers of My Celebrity Closet are mad about our app now, seeing an exclusive collection with a big-name retailer is only going to get them even angrier. A fight that will likely leave one of us bruised and out-of-business seems inevitable.

Tuesday, December 12

3:25 p.m.

I'll spare the little details of my day. It was 8 full hours of worrying about the meeting with the attorney.

My mom is home from work. She took a half day to be here to help me understand everything. She's making French press coffee and straightening up the living room. I decide to light some candles. But then I don't. Because is it weird to light candles when you're attorney is dropping by? Is it more weird that I even have an attorney?

3:52 p.m.

Spoiler alert: I still haven't met with Rabia, but in a completely crazy twist, I find out that she has a daughter. That may seem random—but her daughter is THE Style Tiger! I want to text Emma right away. But first, the lawsuit.

5:14 p.m.

The meeting lasts for 61 minutes and we talk about a million things. The most important thing: The attorney says there's absolutely nothing for us to worry about. She says it's completely bizarre and out of the ordinary for a company to send a cease and desist letter like this, especially when our app existed first and has propriety features that are nothing like this other app. She had looked into the company, and it was really new. She said it smells of something fishy. (I loved it when she said that.) We don't need to delete our app, and in the meantime, she'll respond to the attorney who sent the letter and get him to back off.

Before Rabia left, my mom does something totally embarrassing. She tells the attorney that my friends and I are huge fans of Style Tiger and maybe her daughter could sign something and send it to us. Why is this the time that my mom has to be all shameless?

"Sure," Rabia says. "Can you stop by tomorrow, Charlie? We live in Chelsea. I want to go over the letter with you before I send it. You can take a peek at it and say hi to Marianna if you'd like, too."

The Style Tiger = Marianna.

It seems like *everyone online is a little bit fake.* Knowing that suddenly fills a patch that has been causing me to punish myself since the situation with Seven, like I should have seen or anticipated his phoniness. Everyone online is a little bit fake. I say it again and continue to feel even better.

"I would love that," I say.

Running a business is not easy, but it's great to have a support system. I'm learning that it's key to focus on what you do well (for me, that's coding) and allow yourself to ask for help with the stuff you're not so great at. If I tried to deal with this lawsuit myself, it would be a disaster. It's smarter for my business to allow the experts to take care of it. I'm not happy about dealing with a situation like this, but I feel a little glimmer of pride on how I'm stepping up and dealing with it.

6:23 p.m.

So much has been going on that I completely forgot about the voting for the awards, at least for the past eight hours, which is actually a long time in this case. I check out the website and don't see anything posted. I do see that voting is open for one more day. I must have gotten the dates mixed up. This means no news anytime soon.

Wednesday, December 13

4:02 p.m.

Before I go to Rabia's apartment, I stop off at Posman Books in Chelsea Market to grab a copy of a new fashion book that just came out called *The 2.0s*. It's about the next generation of fashion models, and I know Emma will love it. That's what I'm going to have Style Tiger sign for her.

But is it lame that I'm asking Style Tiger (Marianna? I'm not sure what I should call her at this point) for her autograph? She might even be annoyed that her mom offered her up to do this. But, no turning back now.

4:30 p.m.

I ring the doorbell at exactly 4:30 p.m. I wanted to be two minutes early, but the elevator in the building goes too slowly. To my surprise, Marianna opens the door. A little black dog follows behind her. She says hello and immediately starts talking like she was expecting me and we've been friends forever.

"This actually isn't my dog, but I'm pet-sitting for my next-door neighbor," she says.

Famous Instagrammers—they're just like us.

I'm trying to remember every single thing I see so that I can report back to Emma. Marianna (she introduces herself that way at the door so that's what I'm going with—it would be weird to call someone by their social media handle anyway) has on white-and-silver Yeezys. The apartment smells like eucalyptus, which I'm not sure is coming from her perfume or a candle that's burning in the entryway. She's carrying her laptop and there's a sticker of a mermaid on the front. In the hallway, there's a hard-shell pink suitcase in sight, which Marianna explains is because she's going on a work trip to San Francisco with her mom.

She's still talking about Hercules (the dog) when she pauses for a second, and I realize that I haven't officially introduced myself.

"Oh, and by the way, I'm Charlie," I say confidently but not boldly. There's a difference and I'm working on the latter. And to try and distract from my sudden, awkward introduction, I keep talking. "You mentioned you're going to San Francisco. I might be headed there, too." I stop myself from explaining any more, as it feels like I may jinx our chance of going to the awards just by bringing it up. I hope she won't ask any questions about it.

"Cool. Do you want something to drink?"

"Yeah, that would be great." Marianna is easy and friendly, but I'm still uncomfortable. There are rules when interacting with social media stars and celebrities, and I don't know what they are. I'm not sure if I'm supposed to hang out with Marianna for this long or whether I should ask if her mom is around. I don't want Marianna to feel like she has to entertain me. And everything feels so effortless and casual that asking for an autograph suddenly seems like a jarring intrusion of privacy, like I'm a groupie that has infiltrated her life behind a filter.

She pops open two fizzy organic sodas, and I realize how blunt her bangs are—not the wispy kind that most girls have. She must have the confident *and* bold thing figured out.

I'm still trying to decide whether I should ask if her mom is home when Rabia walks in from another room.

"How are you feeling today?" She's talking to me. "You must have been in such shock to receive a letter like that." Before I can answer, she keeps talking. She speaks quickly and fills the air with so many words, it seems like silence is something that is extinct here.

"You're in a good position. Everything the letter said is entirely unfounded. I had a completely hectic morning, so I haven't had a chance to write up the draft just yet. I'll email it to you for your approval before I send it. It should scare them off."

She keeps talking. Her theory is that it might have been the girls from the soccer team. "It clearly was someone unprofessional because of the way the letter was written," she says. "You mentioned that you were having some problems with them, so they could have been behind it. It also could have been completely random. Sometimes scam artists will create bogus businesses that mirror new, on-the-rise companies and try to scare them out of staying in business by claiming copyright infringement. Then they fill the hole you leave behind. Or they just try to get money from you and never have any intention of starting a company. Your app has gotten a lot of buzz recently, especially with being nominated for a Tech&Innovation Award, so it doesn't seem like a coincidence that this is all happening now."

She pauses and takes a breath. "It also could have been something completely harmless. If the company is international, they may just not have an understanding of copyright laws." She says the attorney listed on the letter appears to be based in the U.S., but that the website for their law firm is a bit odd and has a few different locations listed, some of them overseas.

"Or it could have been someone trying to scare you out of your competition," Marianna says. I almost forgot she was there and that I still need to find a way to ask her for her autograph. It's an out-there idea, and the way she says it is almost like she doesn't mean it—but more of a way to break up her mom's rambling with a thought of her own.

Who knows, but the subject quickly changes anyway.

Marianna pulls out her phone and shows me that she's already downloaded The Fashionist. It never gets old seeing our app live in the wild.

"I'm pretty much obsessed with it because I don't always have time to put together looks," she says. "I get so much stuff from fashion companies that I even forget what's in my own closet. This keeps my content fresh and saves me some time. I may be running a brand, but it's not like my biology teacher understands and lets me skip out on tests."

I feel you, is what I want to say.

"Look, the outfit I put together yesterday was created using your app," she says, pointing at a square picture on Instagram. She's wearing wide-legged black pants with a camel-colored velvet bodysuit. "I just posted it today and tagged you."

"I'm so happy you love it," I say. "We're nominated for a Tech&Innovation Award. We're just waiting to see how the voting shakes out."

"Oh, I'll totally tell my followers to vote for you." She's already tapping on her phone before her sentence is completely finished.

I need to head out in order to have enough time to finish my homework. Knowing that she used the app and doesn't just see me as an awkward girl standing in her apartment, I decide to ask her to sign the book I got for Emma. She says she's happy to do it.

"Hey Emma! I absolutely adore you and your amazing fashion sense! X–The Style Tiger"

As I leave her apartment, it's snowing but doesn't feel crazy cold. I will associate this exact temperature and scene with the feeling of being over-the-moon for the rest of my life. The attorney is taking care of the rogue company. Our line with Urban Outfitters is happening. Seven could move to an island in the Caribbean or get nominated for the Tech&Innovation Awards—I truly don't care. And not only did Marianna sign a book for Emma, she's about to blast out to her fans that they should all vote for The Fashionist. I think it's safe to say I'm about to surprise Emma with the best gift ever.

14,690 downloads. A new record. Thanks, Marianna.

So this is what relief feels like?

There are a lot of highs and lows when running a business. You are building something from scratch and it takes a lot of work. But this feels especially good because the app is unique to us—we developed it together as a reflection of something we love and care about. No one can take that from us.

Thursday, December 14

9:15 a.m.

In the middle of my science teacher reading us a passage about homeostasis, I'm reading an email—*The* Email—from the Tech&Innovation Awards team.

• • • • • • • • • • • • • • • • • •

Dear Tech&Innovation Awards Candidate:

We sincerely appreciate you submitting your app for consideration. After a very close number of votes, we are very happy to tell you that you have made it into the top three. Our travel coordinator will be in touch to provide details on getting to San Francisco. Look forward to meeting you then to determine the final winner.

The Tech&Innovation Awards Team

• • • • • • • • • • • • • • • • • •

I read it six times.

And then I read it six more times.

And I wanted to read it six more times.

This is the exact opposite of homeostasis—my whole world just changed.

I realize I should probably let the rest of The Fashionist team know the news. I grab my phone and I am about to click on the group text when it hits me that it would be so much more fun to announce the news in person. We're having a Fashionist holiday party next Thursday, right before Christmas school break. Giving them the news then will be the best gift ever. I'll just tell them that I got the dates mixed up and that we'll actually hear something next Friday.

I text the group. At least, I think I do. My phone is slid under my desk so the teacher doesn't see it, and I can barely see the screen to see whose name I'm typing:

ME: We'll know the finalists next Friday.

I think I see Emma's name flash on my screen—I must have gotten it right.

EMMA: Seriously? I cannot wait!

AISHA: So close, yet so far!

10:00 a.m.

Maybe my plan will backfire if the finalists are posted on the website? I check and so far nothing. I decide it's worth taking the chance.

10:10 a.m.

San Francisco!

San Francisco!

San Francisco!

I got a follow-up email with the official invitation attached, including the program. The awards are in the first half of January and our travel will be covered for four days and three nights. We're staying at the Hotel Zeppelin, which is also where the awards ceremony will be held. The itinerary says each team has to give one final presentation to the judges, followed by a lunch, and then the winners will be announced the next day at a special ceremony.

11:15 a.m.

I have to tell someone the news, so I text my mom. She responds right away. She says she's so excited for me, I can probably hear her scream through the text. I want to tell her there is something that shows what you're feeling without words—an emoji. My saltiness is put in check when she also tells me that she'll follow up with the attorney to see where everything stands, so we can get everything resolved before San Francisco.

It's happening. But it almost feels cruel that I'm keeping it to myself, especially given the frantic, antsy state of our group text:

AISHA: How long does it take to tally votes that are digital?

Everyone follows up with sad emojis—including me.

3:00 p.m.

I spend the whole day daydreaming about what San Francisco must be like. I can't wait to see the Golden Gate Bridge, hang out in the Mission District, and buy fancy coffee and pastries at Mr. Holmes Bakehouse. I also try really hard to avoid Emma, Aisha, River, and Jack. I feel like if they get a glimpse of my face, it will tell them everything.

We're going to San Francisco.

They'll know even if my lips never move.

When the bell rings, it's my lifesaver. I don't have to worry about bumping into anyone, and I also finally have free reign to do whatever I want on my phone. I follow every single lifestyle Instagrammer from San Francisco that I can. Then I start making a list of all the restaurants, selfie spots, and boutiques that we need to visit while we're in town.

I also see the attorney has finalized the letter and sent it to my mom and me:

• •

Dear Mr. Pithon,

I am writing on behalf of my client, The Fashionist, regarding your letter of December 8, in which you assert that my client has engaged in an infringement of intellectual property rights.

Given that my client's app was developed and live in the App Store before the

My Celebrity Closet app, your assertions of infringement are totally without merit. Moreover, it is clear that the two apps have a completely different look and feel, and we are confident that any comparison of the key pieces of the code for the two apps would establish that they are entirely different.

As an additional matter, your client's assertions completely disregard the fact that there is no copyright protection for mere concepts or ideas: Only concrete designs are eligible for copyright protection. In this instance, the fact that the design of the My Celebrity Closet app is so commonplace that no copyright is possible. In any event, even if my client had assumed that the My Celebrity Closet app was protected by copyright, there are no intellectual property type characteristics that are similar to The Fashionist app owned by my client.

On behalf of my client we demand that you and your client immediately cease and desist from any continued baseless accusations and demands of this nature. If your client fails to do so and we are forced to take legal action, we will seek not only damages but our attorneys' fees. We also will seek our attorneys' fees should we be forced to respond to any legal actions taken by your client.

Sincerely yours,

Rabia Hewitt
Managing Partner
The Law Offices of Hewitt and Feldman LLP

She includes a separate note to me that this should be the last we hear from this company. I hope whoever sent this letter spends a few nights tossing and turning in bed after reading what my lawyer sent—just like I did.

Thursday, December 21

5:38 p.m.

I manage to keep the secret all week, and by some holiday miracle nothing has been posted online. The good luck only needs to last a few more minutes since the party is about to begin.

River arrives first, Emma and Aisha arrive together just a few minutes later, and then Jack walks in looking super distracted, but then I'm distracted because Aisha wants to do gifts right away. "I can't wait any longer," she says. You have no clue, I think.

Everyone starts passing out presents and I give Emma the book with the Style Tiger's autograph. She rips it open and as soon as she sees the face of Gigi Hadid, she starts freaking out. "I've been wanting this book. Thank you, Charlie. This is absolutely amazing."

"Well, open it up," I tell her.

"Oh, did you write me a love letter?" Her cheeks are rosy, and I know it's a sign of her happiness. Then, as she opens the book, I watch the color drain completely away and her face go white as she sees the autograph. That's also a sign of happiness.

"What in the world, Charlie?" Emma asks in disbelief, as she realizes the inside contains the Style Tiger's autograph along with a personal message. "Is this real?"

I explain that our attorney is actually the Style Tiger's mom.

"I've never been so happy to be threatened with a lawsuit before," Emma says. We all laugh. "Sorry, everyone, I think my gift is the winner this year."

"Actually, maybe not," I say. Everyone sort of looks at me with doubt. "Remember when I told you that nominations weren't announced yet?"

Emma says yes, but no one else budges.

"Well, we're actually in the top three," I say. Still, no one moves, so I try to add to the oomph that my lackluster speech fails to convey. "We did it. We're going to San Francisco!"

River sticks her fist in the air, and it seems to break through whatever had everyone else stuck in place. Emma and Aisha squeal and scream and almost kick over the table with the Jingle Juice punch.

"I had this whole thing planned out to give you all envelopes and each one was going to have a clue, but I just couldn't hold it in anymore," I say. Then I explain about when I found out and that I still didn't know which apps from the list have made the cut.

Everyone is so loud with excitement that even Finn looks in and offers us congratulations. Jack is still quiet. It's the kind of unbelievable news that can leave you in disbelief, so I don't really think anything about it.

We all realize it's late, so to get home by curfew (yeah, our parents still gave us a lame curfew on our holiday party night), everyone starts packing up. In a few weeks, we'll all be packing up to head to San Francisco for the awards—an award we may even win.

Jack kind of hangs back, which I don't realize until he's the only one left in the room. I start to get a little panicky. Is he going to bring up the conversation we had about dating again? Maybe he's not OK hanging out with me as friends after all?

"I'm so excited for us, but I do have to tell you something," he says.

My shoulders tense up, ready to block whatever it is that he has to say.

"I know all about that lawsuit," he says. "I'm so glad that your attorney handled it, but I was actually at Seven's house with my dad and I saw a piece of paper on Seven's desk."

"What do you mean? I ask it even though I know what he means.

"I think Seven was trying to scare you out of participating in the awards by creating some fake lawsuit," Jack explains. "I don't know everything. I didn't ask him about it. But I know enough that I had to say something."

The Style Tiger—oh, Marianna—was right, or at least the basis of her idea was. Seven had tried to sabotage us. "So does that mean he's going to be there?

"Yeah, I guess he did make it into the finals," Jack says. "I didn't want to say it in front of everyone, especially because I wasn't even sure that we had made it in. I hate knowing all this stuff. I wish I didn't even know Seven."

I know the feeling.

I had read online that San Francisco can go from bright and sunny one minute to gloomy and gray the next. Over 3,000 miles away in New York, that's exactly what happened in my world.

I'm not bossy, I'm the boss

Beyoncé

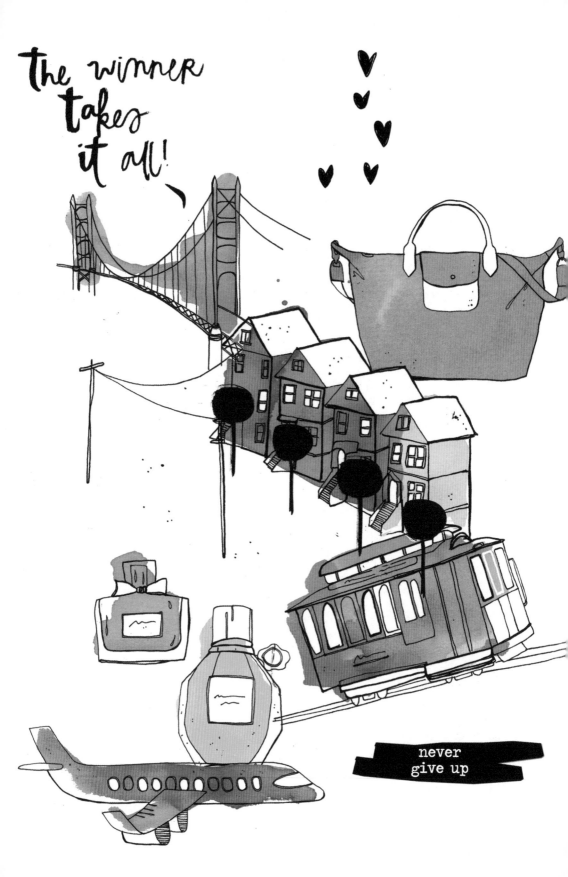

#Big

6:20 a.m.

Once we all found out we were going to San Francisco, we become obsessed with trying to put a more definitive definition of what four weeks actually means: After the holidays. After Mrs. Gridden has her baby and the hot substitute teacher has started. After Emma's aunt's 62nd birthday. After the high school's New Year's Eve party.

Now, it's time.

I'm up and already at the airport.

7:40 a.m.

The airport feels like this bubble of a land that isn't completely real. It's not necessarily where you are anymore but also not where you're going. Maybe that's why people do weird things that they'd never do in real life. We do.

We stop at a perfume booth and spray ourselves with Viktor & Rolf Flowerbomb and Miss Dior—a combination so terrible I'm not sure they're even going to allow us on the plane. We buy more bags of candy than we even want. And because sleep suddenly feels like a new concept that we need to figure out how to do, we each splurge on a leopard-print neck pillow for the cross-country flight.

There are people everywhere who are going everywhere. But for us, it feels like there's only one place to go—San Francisco.

8:36 a.m.

Our plane, which Jack calls a "skyrider" is parked at the gate and boarding has begun. I think about where I would be if I were in the outside world. Aka class. But luckily, our parents persuaded our teachers to let us get out of school for a few days. It took a lot of persuasion. School administrators had three meetings before they finally agreed to it. In the letter I submitted to them for the final meeting, I made it clear that technology isn't just silly Snapchat filters. It's

Spotify and Lyft and virtual reality that allows students to visit the pyramids without ever stepping foot in Egypt. It's a world of apps that better your mental health, allow you to shop for groceries, and capture memories that will last you a lifetime. Technology touches a little bit of everything.

8:47 a.m.

Our group boarding number still hasn't been called. Jack's been on his phone the entire time we've been at the airport. I can't help but wonder if he's sharing secret intel with Seven (who is traveling separately with his mom, and not with Jack). After he told me he knew about the lawsuit, he eventually ended up telling everyone in the group. Even though no one's saying it, there's a fear that Jack might be sharing more with Seven than what we think. Except for River, who's known him forever and trusts him completely.

And honestly, she's probably right. Since getting accepted into the Tech&Innovation Awards, our app has been skyrocketing in popularity. We have so many downloads I can't even keep track of the number anymore (okay, maybe we're up to 112,389), and pages and pages of great reviews. If Jack wanted to sabotage us, he would have done it already.

8:59 a.m.

I'm finally sitting down in seat 23B, which is between Emma and Aisha. River and Jack are sitting right behind us. I hope this isn't the Universe naturally separating us into groups. Us versus Them.

- More paranoia than fact.
- Our parents are a few rows up.

I check my phone one final time to see that our Instagram page is filled with messages from users of The Fashionist wishing us luck at the awards. All the happy vibes.

9:12 a.m.

As the plane takes off, I can feel it rising—up, up, up. It feels like that's what we're destined for, too—to go up, up, up.

Only 5 hours and 43 minutes and we'll be there.

9:45 a.m.

Once the plane gets to a certain altitude, the pressure starts to ease from my body—no more popping ears or heavy legs. But the pressure of where I'm headed and what I have to do is just setting in for me. To win the award, I need to kill it on my presentation.

But, public speaking < coding = Charlie.

There was never a truer statement.

11:15 a.m.

Somewhere over the Midwest, I fall asleep for a little bit. It could have been 10 minutes or it could have been an hour. Emma and Aisha are trying to get some studying in while also fielding emails from the Urban Outfitters team—our collaboration is doing really well. River and Jack are both on their computers.

Stranger Things is available to watch on the tiny plane monitor, and I really want to see it. But I decide to practice for my big presentation instead. Boss move.

12:15 p.m.

We've landed and performed a traveling magic trick—time has gone backward. Now that we're on the West Coast, it's 3 hours earlier. If only we had actually gone into the future—not the past—so I would know if we won the award or not.

1:04 p.m.

We hop in a Lyft and head to the hotel. Jack is in a different car since he has to stay with his family—yes, including Seven—at a different hotel. He looks so miserable about splitting up that I feel silly for doubting his loyalty to the team.

We drive along water that looks blue until you stare at it long enough that it suddenly becomes green. I guess that's the magic of the West Coast. In New

York, the East River always looks brown and muddy no matter how long you look at it. I try to play it cool when we see the Golden Gate Bridge, like it's no big thing. But OMG—we just drove by the Golden Gate Bridge! I think I see a building that was on the show *Silicon Valley* and another one that I read about on a blog, about a house where a bunch of tech people live together and create apps. The bottom of the house looks abandoned with boarded-up windows and red bars on the door. It has to be it.

1:52 p.m.

When I step out of the car and into the hotel is when I first feel it. This is really happening. I'm in San Francisco where so many amazing things happen—and I'm part of it. Maybe I'll even be the next amazing thing that happens here. It's thrilling enough that I want to shout it from a rooftop, but unnerving enough that my stomach wants to empty itself on the sidewalk.

Since the presentations aren't until 11 a.m. tomorrow, we have the rest of the day to settle in. We all take a walk to the Ferry Building for a late lunch. Emma can't wait to go to Blue Bottle Coffee. I tell myself to relax and enjoy seeing the city. The sky is blue. The air feels like wet foam. Charlie Wyeth developed an amazing app. For right now, it's all true.

9:23 p.m.

To touch my nerves would be to touch electricity. But I'm so exhausted from getting up so early, and it's actually past midnight back in New York, that I collapse in bed and fall asleep somewhere in the air before my head even hits the pillow.

Thursday, January 11

7:45 a.m.

Rise, but no shine. The sky is deeply gray. Things have changed. My head is dizzy and my body feels like it's filled with ants, jittery and anxious. The pressure is real.

We all get ready together, Emma puts on a shade of coral lipstick. Aisha uses our app to pick out her outfit. We added a feature right before we left where you can create a capsule wardrobe—like what you have packed in a suitcase.

River's laptop is closed and she's zoning out, instead. "I love hotel beds," she says. "They're basically like clouds in a room."

It sounds like magic. I wish that I hadn't been so tired last night and so stressed this morning, so I could have actually enjoyed it a bit.

"Let's order room service tomorrow morning to celebrate our win," Aisha says. Her comment is like a dart that hits me with anxiety. There are other options besides us winning—like us losing.

"What do you think this event is going to be like?" Emma asks as she walks back into the room, almost ready to go. "Do you think it's going to be full of a bunch of boring nerds?"

"We are boring nerds," River chimes in.

"I think we need some questions as icebreakers so we have something to say," Aisha suggests. So as we finish doing final bits of prep—Emma choosing between a cream cross-body bag and a navy backpack and River starfishing one final time on the sheets—we come up with some go-to questions:

- Where did you travel from?
- What is your app called?
- What code do you like to program in?
- If you could work for any of the tech companies, which one would you choose?

9:01 a.m.

We eat breakfast downstairs at the hotel restaurant. I'm starving, so I pile my plate high with pancakes, a chunk of scrambled eggs, and fresh fruit, and grab a yogurt. As I walk to the table where everyone's sitting, I tell myself that I'll practice my presentation after I'm done eating. But at the thought of the presentation, I'm no longer hungry.

The waitress tells us that Kylie Jenner just left the restaurant. Apparently she's in town because her sister Kim Kardashian West is being honored at another tech conference that's going on. It would be pretty cool to see her, but honestly, I want to spot someone big in tech. Maybe Tim Cook of Apple? Or Sheryl Sandberg of Facebook?

I look out the window and see a tiny storefront that's overflowing with gorgeous green, purple, and pink-striped flowers. I see a giant building in the background that looks like a jumbo concrete pencil. There are steep hills and tiny cars on them that look like they're ready to topple right off the side of the hill. I wonder if I could ever live here. If I could eat in cute restaurants where everyone is wearing cute sneakers. Have an apartment that sits a few stories up from the street. Become a regular at the corner bodega where I buy my sparkling water and a bouquet of flowers wrapped in brown paper.

Emma is taking notes on every girl that walks by. The style here isn't totally different from the style in New York but there are little tweaks. Emma wants to create new inspiration boards and blog posts based on our time here. I'm focused on the presentation, and she's focused on getting us new content. It almost brings me comfort—there is life beyond this competition.

10:17 a.m.

It's getting closer to the time of our awards presentation, and we're all beginning to wonder where Jack is. We're supposed to go together to the room where the presentations are being held. I tell myself that his family probably just wants him around. But I can't help but wonder what Seven may have up his sleeve and whether Jack could be a part of it.

10:37 a.m.

We walk through the hotel, and every time my feet hit the floor I say another word of my presentation to myself. I've memorized it by heart and could probably say it backward at this point. But I have no clue what will happen when I get in front of a giant room of people. I could forget everything, like I never even had a presentation at all.

10:41 a.m.

A text from Jack:

JACK: Hey Charlie, I'm on my way over!

ME: Everything OK?

JACK: We can talk when I get there.

Well, that doesn't sound good. Why would Jack send that to me right before it's time to give my presentation? It's like he wants to get into my head. It's pretty ridiculous that I have to compete against the person who tried to topple my business in the first place.

10:43 a.m.

We take the elevator up to the executive boardroom on the 6th floor. As I step out, I see a life-size peace sign on the wall made of reclaimed wood, red ottomans, and exposed lightbulbs hanging from the ceiling. I think I see one of the bay bridges through the window, but the fog is hugging everything so tightly I can't even be sure the water is what I'm seeing. I don't see Seven or the other teams yet. I'm sure of that.

The woman who is checking everyone in lets me know that after each team is done giving their presentation, lunch will be served on the roof. It makes me feel good to hear the words "after each team is done giving their presentation." It reminds me that this part won't last forever. But for right now, every cell in my body is shaking. Is that a thing? Because it certainly feels like it.

10:55 a.m.

The fashion wearables team, Tauble, arrives. They're nice, and we all say hello to each other. They're all from San Francisco and have actually been nominated for a Tech&Innovation Award before in a different category. I'm distracted by how much older than me they look. Years of experience to my months.

Still no sight of Seven.

10:57 a.m.

The door to the conference room is made of glass, and I can see the space where in just a few short minutes I will be giving our presentation. It isn't set up like a typical conference room with a giant table and a bunch of floating faces positioned around it. The room is large, and even though it's square, chairs are set up in a snail-like shape, circling around the spot where each person will present. It feels like a particularly stressful set-up, like there's no part of me that wouldn't be exposed. Filling the chairs will be the judges, along with other notable voices in the tech industry, and, of course, all of the teams.

I feel terrified. I want to tell The Fashionist team that we should just forget about the competition and head back to New York where we have a successful app and a partnership with Urban Outfitters. *We're already winners there,* I say in a sort of lame voice to myself.

But I'm not running out of the room. I'm not grabbing Emma by the sleeves and telling her to follow me. I'm standing by the door trying to recite my presentation in my head. My sentences are collapsing and my thoughts are evaporating out of my mind. Everything I want to say in the presentation is suddenly unclear. But somehow, the elaborate plan my brain is cooking up to get me out of here is clear, detailed, and thoughtful.

Before I can tell myself to focus, as if there's some other me inside of me that I need to take control of, I see Jack's eyes go wide and I know.

Seven.

He walks in without any fanfare. He has a backpack on that looks like it's probably carrying his laptop. The same laptop that he used to communicate with me and tell me things when he was really asking. I'm pretty sure his hair is some shade of brown, but it's hidden under a black baseball cap that's pulled down close to his eyes. He has on jeans and a dressier shirt. He wants to look low-key but I know the truth: He's viscous and is out for blood.

I'm pretty sure there's something I should say to him. That I should raise my voice and try to embarrass him in front of everyone. To accuse him, shame him, and punish him. But I don't. I'm not going to let him be a distraction anymore.

I, too, want to win.

11:00 a.m.

I was so pulled into the orb that is Seven, that I almost didn't realize we were being called into the room. It's time for the presentations to begin.

The judges include the head of the products team at Apple, Rob Brighten, director of fashion partnerships at Instagram, Eva Chen, the CEO of Stitch Fix, Katrina Lake, and Phillip Picardi, previously chief content editor at *Teen Vogue* and now editor-in-chief at *Out*.

Tauble goes first and talks about the history of their brand and how much they've disrupted the idea of tech as a piece of your wardrobe that's just as essential as socks. It's not just watches—it's everything. Jackets that have buttons to keep you warm in the winter. An earring that can be tapped to call 911 if you're in danger. They just released an app so you can shop their products. I'm so impressed.

Everyone is. The room is clapping loudly as they finish.

Seven is next. There was a time when all I wanted was to meet Seven in person. That time is long gone. But I still can't wait to hear what he sounds like, what kind of demeanor he possesses, and honestly, how he stands up in a room full of tech geniuses and takes credit for my code. My heart is beating so loud, I'm sure that everyone can hear it.

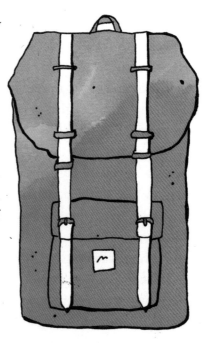

He begins his presentation by giving his name, Theo Seven. He talks about how he has always dreamed of going to Stanford and majoring in computer science. He said he created his app to free up people's time, painting it like some sort of herculean humanitarian effort. His words sort of jumble together, like he's trying to blend his lies into truth. I thought I would be starstruck when I saw him. But I feel nothing until I realize that nothing feels, well, really good.

Now it's my turn.

I walk to the spot where I'm supposed to give my presentation and prepare myself to fail. As I take the final steps, I think of Seven's speech. I almost feel bad for him as I remember the way his sentences sounded so monotone and dull. He had no passion. But I have plenty, something no one can take from me. So I start speaking—and I use it.

My name is Charlie. A few months ago, I was nothing but a girl who often got mistaken for a boy. I was an imperfect friend, the unwanted member of my school's coding club, and the person who faded into the background every day at school. I always felt like I was on the fringe of high school, like all the good memories and moments were meant for someone else. I was just a spectator.

But then I realized there was something that made me happy. I didn't do it to get attention or because I felt like I was supposed to. I did it because it felt so right, and real, and true to me. It was pretty clear that this was happiness—finding my thing. And for me, that was coding.

At first, I did try to code myself into the cool girl. The person who would develop something that all of the fashionable, popular girls at school would like. I wasn't doing it for attention as much as I wanted to impress the friend I already had. Insecure, much? But the deeper I got into creating The Fashionist, an app that helps you pick out your very best outfits so you can feel like the very best version of yourself, I realized it wasn't about that at all.

It became a way for me to spend time with my best friends, spark my confidence, and an outlet to express who I truly am. And along the way, I made more friends and began to stand out at school. Although I will proudly say that I am still not the "cool girl."

But even if that didn't happen, it wouldn't have mattered anyway. Because what I realized is that I found my calling, and it manifested itself in really impressive ways. Today, The Fashionist has gained the attention of major retailers. We recently signed an agreement with Urban Outfitters to create a capsule collection, which sold out shortly after. We have over 156,000 users and we continue to grow.

Getting here wasn't easy. I lied to my friends, family, and many others, and made choices that I might not make now. I was also lied to. I learned that not everyone wants to use their skills for good. But I'm standing up here because I do. I want to continue to expand on The Fashionist and use the funds from this award to not only grow my company and employ more girls, but also to set up coding camps for the imperfect friends, the unwanted members of the school coding club, and the girls who fade into the background.

Everyone always told me about my first love—I pictured a guy with a slight Harry Styles resemblance. But it was nothing like that. Because my very first love was myself. And that's what The Fashionist has turned into, a love letter to myself, but I hope that it can be something that brings you a lot of happiness and joy, too. We all deserve it."

And just like that, it's over. I walk back to my chair feeling as squishy, queasy, and jellylike as I did when I first walked in. But this time I'm smiling because I feel all of those things in the best of ways.

11:57 a.m.

"Holy crap, Charlie—you killed it," Emma shrieks as I take my seat next to her. She's so loud, I'm sure the judges heard her. But then I realize everyone is on their feet clapping—and the only thing anyone can hear is a room filled with the thunder of hands in unison. For me.

12:17 p.m.

The judges thank us for coming and for dedicating so much of our time. They compliment our presentations and say they're looking forward to spending more time with us at the lunch.

We all take the elevator to the private luncheon. As we're going up, it truly feels like I'm hovering above it all. I'm trying to get close enough that I can soak it in. The room where we're eating is incredible. There are all sorts of selfie spots, a giant coloring-book wall, posters with graphic illustrations hanging from the ceiling, and neon signs. There are so many amazing things, I'm not even sure what to put in my story first.

Somehow all of the members of the judging team are already in the room. They are standing near a table full of pineapples with bright straws coming out of the top—inside are coconut pineapple slushies. I'm not sure if I want to go over and talk to them because they're talking to Tauble, and Seven isn't that far away. One more day and you won't have to see him ever again, I tell myself. And so I decide to go over and snag one of the Insta-worthy pineapple drinks.

As I'm waiting for the girl to stick in the straw, I feel a tap on my hand. I look over expecting to see my mom, or Emma, or Aisha, or Jack, or River—but it's Seven. It's the closest we have ever been to each other. I don't feel weak in the knees. I feel bubbles of anger. I have gone over this moment for months, but with Seven right in front of me, he doesn't feel worth even a word. So I say nothing, which feels like exactly what he deserves.

"I guess we're finally getting our time to talk," he says. He lacks the allure and mystery that he seems to have online. He almost seems goofy and unsure of himself.

I sip on the drink, sweet and tropical, and see Emma's shimmery gold top from the corner of my eye.

"I knew you'd be mad. I get it. I wanted to explain myself to you, but it didn't feel possible. But now that you're standing in front of me, I do want you to know that I wasn't trying to steal your code. I was already working on something similar, which is why I had so many questions. I know how it looks. But it's a coincidence. There's room for both of us."

He says it with a bit of a smirk, and I know he's not being genuine. He may suck at being original and coming up with good code, but he's a great manipulator. At least, he used to be.

"You did steal my code," I say. I feel happy that those are the first words I say to Seven IRL. It makes it clear that Seven no longer has any power over me and that I'm really not worried about what he thinks.

"You never said that you were working on an app like mine and you had many chances to. You presented yourself as someone who just wanted to help, but you were using me to better your ideas. That's the truth, and it's very black and white—I know because I looked at the code. It was exactly the same as mine. We happen to be in the same place right now, but I'm here to compete, not talk to you. For months you hid behind your computer screen and that used to bother me, but now I know it's exactly where I like you—where I can't see you and can forget that you exist."

It takes all of three minutes for me to spit Seven out like a seed.

I walk away, and unfortunately leave my pineapple drink behind. For a second I feel like maybe I was too harsh. But then I remember how vindictive Seven had been, how much he had truly taken from me—stealing my ideas and rushing to get the app into the App Store before mine. And to make it even worse, he tried to come up with a fake lawsuit to get me to drop out of the awards. I deserve to stand up for myself, and that's exactly what I did.

As I continue the walk back to my team, the room almost feels as if it's starting to tilt. I had been dreading running into Seven and for months had stressed over the fact that he had even been nominated. I had believed that I would see him and fall into the trance of his soft, doughy eyes as he sweetly called me "Charlie Girl." For months, that's what I thought. And after our interaction I realized that, for months, that's what he thought would happen, too.

"Oh my God, tell us everything," Emma says as I approach her, Aisha, River, and Jack.

"We were seriously about to come over and rescue you," River says. It was the softest, nicest thing I'd ever heard her say.

"It was nothing, really." I tell them what Seven said and how he tried to get me to forgive him, but that I wasn't having it. "We don't need to talk about it anymore. It was something annoying that happened but I want to enjoy this experience. Let Seven sit over there and sulk and hope he wins. But let's just forget about winning. Let's savor this."

"So you're just going to let him get away with this?" River seems disappointed. It wasn't the response I expected.

"He basically stole our code and created a fake company to try and prevent us from showing up, and you aren't going to say anything to the judges?" River asked again, more forcefully than I had ever heard her.

"We're already here," I say. "There's no reason to give him any more power over us. We're moving on. Our presentation and app will speak for themselves."

"Charlie's right," Jack adds. "Even if we get Seven disqualified, then what? We've already made our presentation and I truly feel that we're going to win. Sorry, Charlie. I've actually been trying to warn you that I thought he was going to try and talk to you. I just had a feeling."

That explains the distance.

"Let's not argue," Emma interjects. "He wants to tear us apart. It's his last attempt to try and win something."

"I guess," River says. "But I'm just annoyed that he's even here. He doesn't deserve it."

"He doesn't deserve it," I say. "He also doesn't deserve our attention."

River nods in agreement.

Suddenly Aisha breaks up the conversation. "Hey, we have a problem. The app is down."

"See," River says. "We should have taken him down while we could have. Now he's taken us down. Literally."

"Let's not jump to conclusions," I say. "I highly doubt in the five seconds since I walked away from him that he was so angry he shut down our app. Let me look into this."

Inside I was freaking out. If the judges were doing last checks into the apps, they would see that ours wasn't working. It would look really unprofessional. I also didn't want Seven to have the last word.

"Let's get our laptops and we can figure this out together," I say.

River grabs her computer from her bag and we get to work checking out what is wrong.

It could have been Seven's last move, and he might have checkmated us.

1:18 p.m.

It was a stressful 31 minutes. We discovered that someone had hacked into our account and changed all the passwords. It wasn't Seven. River tracked it to a server overseas. Unfortunately, stuff like this happens sometimes, but thankfully, our app is back up now. Never a dull day!

Aisha did some undercover work and says the judges haven't left the front of the room where they have been talking to groups of people. The chances of them looking at our app while it was down were really slim. Crisis averted.

Friday, January 12

8:15 a.m.

We finished out the day yesterday by visiting Alcatraz and taking the ferry to Sausalito for dinner and shopping. The clouds and fog had mostly dissipated by then and the sunshine came down in what looked like wiggly strings the color of bananas. It was a long day, so this morning I'm slow to get up. I grab my phone from under my pillow before my feet even hit the floor and see this text:

"You're all high and mighty, but you're just evil."

It takes me a little sleuthing to figure out who it is, but eventually Jack confirms that it's Seven's number.

But what is he talking about?

9:02 a.m.

I meet up with everyone to go to breakfast at Tartine Bakery, and Jack explains everything. He says Seven's app crashed last night, and apparently in the lines of code there were messages that said "The Fashionist rules" and "#TeamFashionist." I'm speechless. It's impossible. We would obviously never do anything like that.

Jack says he talked to Seven for over 30 minutes and explained that we had nothing to do with it, especially because when it happened we were at Alcatraz and our phones were turned off.

"I'm sure he's made plenty of people angry," Emma says. "He's probably done this to other people and they sought revenge on him."

We walk back to the hotel room to get ready for the awards ceremony. I can't wrap my head around who would do this. First, the page that was created on Facebook to bully me suddenly disappeared and now someone had gone rogue and ruined Seven's code. Somehow the two feel connected. So many different scenarios run through my head. Jack? River? A stranger we met at the Hackathon? None of them seems possible.

As if my thoughts are audible, Emma shares a different theory. "I bet Seven did this and is completely making it up just to get sympathy from the judges."

Seven sabotaging himself? It seems like the most real possibility.

11:45 a.m.

Back at the hotel I change into a short blue dress and put a faux fur jacket on top of it. Both pieces are from our first Urban Outfitters collection. Once I'm ready, I check the App Store to see if Seven's app is back up and running. It is. I'm happy about that. If we beat Seven, I want it to be fair and square.

12:30 p.m.

It's finally time to head to the awards ceremony, which we just found out was moved. It's being held at Katrina Lake's headquarters in Montgomery Tower, which has this nice tech company vibe combined with fashion and style. Just what we love! Sometimes a change of plan is not too bad.

On the way, my dad texts me and reminds me to send him pictures. It feels good to be connected back to New York. I send him a few selfies of me at iconic spots in San Francisco, one of my presentation yesterday, a view of our hotel room, and a blurry shot of the ride as we head off to finally find out who the winner is.

1:01 p.m.

Traffic is a bit of a nightmare. A Google bus had broken down and is blocking all of the lanes. But we finally make our way to the Stitch Fix offices.

I see the judges and a few other familiar faces from yesterday's presentations. I say hello and move a few steps pass them.

59 minutes to go.

1:57 p.m.

Right before the awards are scheduled to begin, everyone starts moving closer to the middle of the floor. I think it's a subtle cue that the awards are about to begin.

I do see a table full of awards. But other than that, no hints.

"I think the last one is ours," Aisha says. "And by the last one, I mean the last one that they'll give out to the winner."

"There's no way to tell," River says. I'm happy for her glass-half-empty attitude in this minute. I don't have to be the one to explain that it's impossible to tell and anything else is only speculation.

Things I think about in this exact second. Our flight leaves tomorrow morning. And the speech is about to begin.

2:01 p.m.

Right on time, Eva Chen opens the awards ceremony with a speech.

"The bar was really high this year," she says.

I know I should be hyper-aware of what she's saying—after all, I have to be ready to take the stage. But all I can think is that she must always say that.

"One of the things that was so great about this pool of competitors was the number of women who made it to this stage, and not just women, but teenage women. We are here to announce the winner, but in that way, we and you are all winners. We all benefit from technology, and it's clear the future is bright. To determine the winner, we based our decision on many factors: innovation, preparedness, passion, input we received from the people who actually used the app, and reliability."

As she says that, I'm pretty sure she looks directly at me. But then her gaze seems to go to Seven and the wearable tech team, too. Maybe she's just looking at everyone in a completely random fashion. She finishes up her thoughts and then picks up the first award from the table.

2:10 p.m.

The thing about time is that it is unchanging. One second will always be one second. One minute, one minute, and one hour, one hour. And yet, time can feel stretchy and moldable as taffy—it can feel long and never-ending or it can feel short and disappearing. The five seconds it took for the judge to pick up the award and start speaking suddenly feels like years. I almost feel the pain of waiting in my bones.

And then she calls our name.

Wait, what does that mean? Does she call the winner first or last? I think she probably explained that but I wasn't paying attention.

I realize looking at River and everyone around me that they don't call the winner first.

We lost.

I could barely get the strength to stand up and walk to the stage.

We lost.

Your app is terrible.

You're terrible.

I'm terrible.

But somehow I have the courage to walk up on stage.

Because our app is amazing.

I'm amazing.

"Charlie, we absolutely loved your app," the judge says. "We were so impressed with how you've taken something and turned it into a successful and multipronged business. I wish we had some eloquent reason why we didn't choose you, but it truly comes down to the fact that competition was tight this year. But we hope that we can make it up to you."

She smiles, and Katrina Lake suddenly comes on the stage. She has on a crisp white shirt and silver mules. Her eyes twinkle and her lips are perfectly pink. She looks like good news.

"I was so impressed with your drive, your spirit, your passion, your smarts, that we at Stitch Fix would like to award you with a one-year residency in our New York offices," she says. "We'll give you a space to work, gift you a $25,000 scholarship, and we would love for you to work with our designers to create a The Fashionist t-shirt for our line that we will also feature on your app."

We are speechless times a thousand.

2:37 p.m.

The final moments of the awards are a blur. I know they announce the winner—the Tauble team. I clap and feel happy for them. I know what it's like to pour yourself into something. At some point, Seven walks out of the room—and that's the last time I see him, eventually only existing in the form of a lesson learned. My guess is that it was the part where the judges started talking about originality and how critical it is to success.

After the awards ceremony is officially done, we all dance arm-in-arm through the store as if we have won the first-place prize. It truly feels like we did. We aren't leaving with a trophy, but we are leaving with a scholarship, a new opportunity, and the respect of those in the industry.

Winning isn't one thing: It's many things. And we did indeed win.

Saturday, January 20

11:30 a.m.

After months of scandals, hard work, and drama, I'm excited for a chill weekend. I have nothing to do on my list except to watch Netflix. I just hopped out of the shower and I hear my mom yell that there's a package for me. I wasn't expecting anything. I throw on an oversized sweater and leggings and hurry downstairs.

It's an all-white box with black letters. It says Stitch Fix on the front. Inside is the Longchamp bag I have been waiting for. It feels as soft as butter. And instead of my mom buying it for me—I earned it.

At the bottom of the bag is a black envelope. I pull out the card.

• • • • • • • • • • • • • • • • • • • •

Dear Charlie,

Just a little gift of gratitude from the Stitch Fix crew. You totally rocked your presentation, and we're excited to support your dreams and work with you over the next year. We believe you represent a new and exciting generation of talented and creative young women working in technology. We're delighted to see you at our office in New York next Monday at 4 p.m.

Lucky us to have you!

Katrina

• • • • • • • • • • • • • • • • • • • •

As I read the words "you represent a new and exciting generation of talented and creative young women in technology," I feel a profound sense of pride. I always felt like I needed a metamorphosis, a change. But now I realize I never needed to change—I just needed to embrace the real me.

3:02 p.m.

20 Facts About Me:

1. I'm 16.
2. People still sometimes think I'm a boy. Probably because my name is Charlie. But also because my profile says I'm a tech entrepreneur. (Hello, tech entrepreneurs can be girls, and Charlies can, too.)
3. I created my very own app, The Fashionist.
4. The thing I love most about myself is that I am a coder.
5. Every selfie I take looks terrible. But I don't care.
6. My first capsule collection with Urban Outfitters sold out.
7. And I'm already working on a second one.
8. The moon fascinates me.
9. My dream job is—the one I am creating for myself.
10. I'm going to be starting my junior year in 4,260 minutes. Less than 72 hours.
11. I know that it's okay not to feel confident 100 percent of the time.
12. I'm obsessed with anything pineapple-flavored.
13. Stitch Fix did throw an awesome party for the the launch of our t-shirt. Really, everybody was there.
14. When I'm stressed, a walk down Spring Street in Soho makes me feel better.
15. Having a boyfriend is not the ultimate goal for me.
16. I would like to read 10 new books this year. #goals
17. I am helping other girls become coders, too!
18. I haven't gone anywhere without my leather tote since I got it.
19. Emma, Aisha, River, and Jack are my best friends.
20. I wish I was—me.

Nothing
about me
right now
is perfect.
But I'm
perfectly
Serena.

Serena Williams

#whatsnext

Want to know more about technology? Do you want to learn how to program and discover everything you are capable of in the world of technology? Are you the next tech hotshot? Will you build your own future? Will you solve the problems in the world with tech? Start your own business? Build the next awesome app? Read this and you'll know what to do next. Girls who code rule the world!

after-School

Girls Who Code
Black Girls Code
CoderDojo
CodeAdvantage® – Girl Code Power
Flatiron School

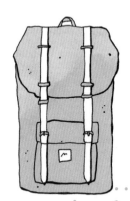

at School

MinecraftEdu
Lego® WeDo
Code.org®

#bethenerd

to do online

Code.org®
Tynker™
Scratch
Codecademy
Made with Code
Swift Playgrounds
Code Avengers
CodeCombat
Khan Academy
Tekkie Uni
Tech Rocket

#letstry

let's do this!

to join

The Hour of Code

robots

Ozobot
Lego® Boost
Sphero
Dash and Dot

#goto

coding camps

Girls Who Code
Kode with Klossy
iD Tech
Alexa Café
DigiGirlz High Tech Camp
Emagination® Tech Camps
Digital Media Academy
CodeREV Kids

YEAH

build
Piper

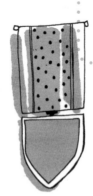

for more coding inspiration

www.thenewgirlcode.com

If you're one of
those people who
has that little
voice in the back
of her mind saying,
'Maybe I could do
[fill in the blank],'
don't tell it to be
quiet. Give it a
little room to grow,
and try to find an
environment it can
grow in.

Reese Witherspoon

there are no limits

go for it!

#Goals

What are your goals in live? What do you want to accomplish? What are your dreams? Think big! Write them down and go for it.

1. Learn to code
2. Think big
3. Start

THINK BIG!

BE creative

be bold
be brave
be amazing
be worthy

Shonda Rhimes

BOSS UP

THiNK BiG!

Nerd?
I prefer the term
intellectual
badass

I LOVE CODING

THE NEW
GIRL CODE

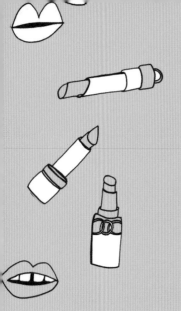

THINK BIG!

you are AMAZING!

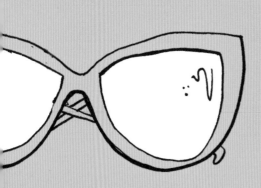